'There is no *this time*. This is just a job for me—that's all. I'm not interested in anything else.'

Everything in Zafir rejected that, and he lifted one hand to cup Kat's delicate jawline. Just the silken brush of her hair against the back of his hand had his body hardening all over again.

'Why are you denying this, Kat? Whatever is between us, it's mutual. And it's even stronger than before.'

She shook her head. 'It's not mutual.'

'Liar…' Zafir breathed as every part of his body went on fire with an urgent and undeniable desire to prove Kat wrong. And along with that desire he felt something much more dangerous: *emotion*.

To block it out, deny it, Zafir cupped his hand behind Kat's neck and drew her into him until he could feel the length of her willowy body pressed against his. And then he bent his head and covered Kat's mouth with his, and for the first time in eighteen months the roaring savage heat inside him was momentarily soothed.

It was so profound and overwhelming that for long seconds Zafir didn't even deepen the kiss. He just relished the sensation of Kat's soft, lush mouth under his. And then she made a soft mewling sound and Zafir fell over the brink of his control and hauled Kat even closer, kissing her deeply enough that he could see stars.

Mills & Boon welcomes you
to the passionate world of Abby Green's

Rulers of the Desert

*These brothers might rule their kingdoms—
but can they rule their own desire?*

Zafir and Salim Al-Noury were born to be kings.
These powerful monarchs have never had their
wishes challenged—until they meet the women
they're determined to take to their beds!

Kat and Charlotte might find their seduction
to be irresistible… But to claim them truly
their seducers must make them their desert queens!

A Diamond for the Sheikh's Mistress

Available now

A Christmas Bride for the King

Coming soon

A DIAMOND FOR THE SHEIKH'S MISTRESS

BY
ABBY GREEN

MILLS
BOON

First Published in Great Britain 2017
By Mills & Boon, an imprint of HarperCollins*Publishers*
1 London Bridge Street, London, SE1 9GF

© 2017 Abby Green

ISBN: 978-0-263-07004-0

MIX
Paper from
responsible sources
FSC
www.fsc.org **FSC® C007454**

This book is produced from independently certified FSC paper
to ensure responsible forest management. For more information
visit www.harpercollins.co.uk/green.

Printed and bound in Great Britain
by CPI Group (UK) Ltd, Croydon, CR0 4YY

Irish author **Abby Green** threw in a very glamorous career in film and TV—which really consisted of a lot of standing in the rain outside actors' trailers—to pursue her love of romance. After she'd bombarded Mills & Boon with manuscripts they kindly accepted one, and an author was born. She lives in Dublin, Ireland, and loves any excuse for distraction. Visit abby-green.com or e-mail abbygreenauthor@gmail.com.

Books by Abby Green

Mills & Boon Modern Romance

Awakened by Her Desert Captor

Wedlocked!

Claimed for the De Carrillo Twins

Brides for Billionaires

Married for the Tycoon's Empire

One Night With Consequences

An Heir to Make a Marriage
An Heir Fit for a King

Billionaire Brothers

Fonseca's Fury
The Bride Fonseca Needs

Blood Brothers

When Falcone's World Stops Turning
When Christakos Meets His Match
When Da Silva Breaks the Rules

Visit the Author Profile page at millsandboon.co.uk for more titles.

CHAPTER ONE

SHEIKH ZAFIR IBN HAFIZ AL-NOURY, King of Jandor, was oblivious to the exquisite mosaics on the path under his feet as he paced restlessly, and he was equally oblivious to the water burbling from the ornate central fountain. The tiny multicoloured birds darting between the lush exotic blooms also went unnoticed in this, just one of the many stunning courtyards of his royal palace in Jahor, the imposing capital city of his kingdom, which ran from snow-capped mountains in the east, across a vast desert to the sea in the west.

Zafir was oblivious to it all because all he could think about was *her*. It was getting worse. He'd had to call an important meeting to a premature end because he'd felt constricted and claustrophobic, aware of the heat in his blood and the ache in his core. An ache he'd largely managed to ignore for the last eighteen months.

Liar, whispered a voice, *those first three months were hell.*

Zafir scowled in remembrance. But then his father had died, and all his time and attention since then had been taken up with his accession to the throne and taking control of his country.

But now it was as if he finally had time to breathe again, and she was back. Infiltrating his thoughts and dreams. Haunting him.

Zafir loosened his robe at his neck with jerky movements. *Sexual frustration*, he told himself, momentarily coming to a halt on the path. It was just sexual frustration. After all, he hadn't taken a woman to bed since... *her*, and that incensed him even more now.

It wasn't due to lack of interest from women. It was due to Zafir's single-minded focus on his job and his commitment to his people. But he was aware of the growing pressure from his council and his people to find a suitable Queen and provide heirs, so they would have faith and feel secure in their King and future.

Zafir issued a loud curse, scattering the birds around him in a flurry. *Enough.* He whirled around and strode back out of the courtyard, determined to set in motion the search for an appropriate match and put *her* out of his head once and for all.

He stopped in his tracks, though, as he passed the overgrown entrance to the high-walled garden nearby. None of the gardeners had touched it in years, and Zafir hadn't had the heart to enforce its clean-up since taking power. He knew that his staff viewed it almost superstitiously; some believed it was haunted.

Maybe it was, he thought bleakly, his thoughts momentarily diverted.

He went and stood at the entrance and looked at the wildly overgrown space and realised with a jolt that today was the anniversary. The anniversary of his sister's death. Nineteen years ago. He'd been thirteen and she'd been just eleven. He stepped in, almost without realising what he was doing.

Unlike the rest of the pristinely manicured grounds, there was no water trickling into the circular pool that could barely be seen under greedy weeds. There were no lush flowers or exotic birds. It was dormant. Still. Dead.

He could still remember hearing the almost otherworldly scream of his brother Salim, Sara's twin. When Zafir had burst into the garden he'd found his brother cradling Sara's limp body, her head dangling over his arm at an unnatural angle. Her face had been whiter than white, her long black hair matted with the blood which had been dripping into the fountain's pool behind them, staining the water.

Salim had screamed at him to do something... *Save her...* But Zafir had known instinctively that she was gone. He'd tried to take Sara out of Salim's arms to carry her into the palace, to find help, see if there was any chance, but Salim, sensing Zafir's grim assessment, had only tightened his hold on his twin sister's body and shouted hoarsely, 'If you can't help, then don't touch her... Leave us alone!'

Sara had died from a massive head and neck injury after falling from the high wall around this garden where they'd used to play and climb, in spite of Zafir's protests. Salim hadn't spoken for weeks afterwards...

To Zafir's shame, the dominating thing he now recalled was the awfully familiar disconnect between him and his siblings. The sense of isolation that had pervaded his whole life. He'd always been envious of Salim and Sara's very special and close bond, which had been to the exclusion of everyone else. But right then he would have gladly given up his own life to see his sister's brought back...

'*Ahem*... Sire?'

Zafir tensed. Very few people managed to catch him unawares and he didn't appreciate this intrusion into such a private moment.

He didn't turn around as he responded curtly, 'Yes?'

There was some throat-clearing. 'The...ah... Heart of Jandor diamond, Sire. There are things we need to discuss about it, and the upcoming diplomatic tour.'

Zafir closed his eyes briefly, letting the painful past fade back to where it belonged, and when he was ready turned around to survey the young aide he'd taken on after his father's death almost fifteen months ago—much to his council's disapproval. They'd wanted him to keep his father's old guard and not rock the boat, but Zafir favoured a more modern outlook for his country's future and was slowly but surely implementing his ways.

He started walking back towards the palace, his aide hurrying alongside him, used to keeping up with his demanding King by now.

The Heart of Jandor diamond was a mythically rare gem. Thought for years to have been either stolen or lost, it had been found recently during archaeological excavations outside the palace walls. There had been much rejoicing and fervent whispering of it being a good omen. It was the largest known red diamond in the world, famed for its beauty. When it had first been discovered it had had a natural heart shape, and so had been cut and refined into its current incarnation, retaining its distinctive shape.

It had originally been unearthed in the eastern mountains of Jandor and given as a gift to woo Zafir's French great-grandmother. The fact that her marriage to his great-grandfather was the only one in his family history which had allegedly been a happy one merely confirmed for Zafir that love within marriage was as much of a rarity as the diamond itself—and about as improbable.

Irritated to find his mind deviating like this, Zafir said now, 'Well? What are your thoughts, Rahul?'

'We are starting the diplomatic tour in New York next week, as discussed.'

New York.

No one else would have noticed the slightest misstep in Zafir's authoritative stride. But *he* noticed. And he despised himself for it. Suddenly all thoughts of his sister and the lingering grief he felt were eclipsed by *her* again. The ease with which she could get to him after all this time only made him angrier.

What the hell was wrong with him today?

Manhattan was primarily where their relationship had played out over several months. And in spite of his best efforts his blood simmered, reminding him of just how far under her spell he'd fallen. Until it had been almost too late.

Zafir's strides got longer, as if he could outrun the past nipping at his heels, but even by the time he'd reached his palatial offices she was still there, those amber-hazel eyes looking up at him slumberously while a sinful smile made that famously sexy and lush mouth curve upwards. As if she'd known exactly what she was doing to him, drawing him deeper and deeper into—

'Sire?'

Zafir gritted his jaw against the onslaught of memories and turned around to focus on his aide. 'Yes, Rahul.'

The young man looked nervous. 'I...ah...have a suggestion to make regarding the jewel.'

'Go on,' Zafir bit out, curbing his impatience. His aide was not to know that he'd unwittingly precipitated the storm currently raging inside him.

'The diamond is being brought on your diplomatic tour as an exhibit and a stunning example of Jandor's many attractions in a bid to promote business and tourism.'

Zafir's impatience spiked in spite of his best efforts. 'I know very well why we're bringing it on the diplomatic tour. It was my idea.'

The man swallowed, visibly nervous. 'Yes, and we'd planned on displaying it in each city in a protected glass case.'

'Rahul...' Zafir said warningly, coming close to the end of his tether.

His aide spoke quickly now. 'The suggestion I want to make is this—rather than show it off in a sterile and protected environment, I thought it might prove to be far more dynamic if it were seen up close... We could let people see how accessible it is and yet still exclusive and mysterious.'

Now he had Zafir's attention. 'What are you talking about?'

'I'm talking about hiring someone—a model—someone who will actually wear the jewel and come with us on the tour. Someone who will walk with us among the guests at each function, so they can appreciate the jewel's full beauty, see how it lives and breathes—just like Jandor's beauty.'

Zafir looked at Rahul for a long moment. This was why he'd hired the younger man after all—to inject new blood into his father's archaic council.

The idea had merit, and Zafir assessed it in seconds. However he was about to dismiss it for various reasons—not least of which were to do with security—but just as he opened his mouth to speak an image exploded into his head, turning his words to dust.

He immediately turned away from the younger man, for fear that something would show on his face. All he could see was *her*, lying on a bed, with her long, sinuous limbs and her treacherously hypnotic beauty, naked but for the jewel that nestled between her high, full breasts. It would glow fiery red against that perfect pale skin.

As red as his blood—which wasn't simmering now. It had boiled over.

He'd allowed the floodgates to open, and right at that moment Zafir knew there was only one way to rid himself of this ache and move on. And he *had* to move on. His country depended on it.

Zafir's mind reeled as the idea took root and embedded itself deep inside him. Was he really considering revisiting the past and the one person he'd vowed never to think or speak of again?

A spurt of rebelliousness and something much more ambiguous ignited inside him.

Why not?

This could be the perfect opportunity to sate his desires before he committed to his full responsibilities and the people of Jandor owned him completely. And there was only one woman Zafir wanted.

She owed him, he told himself grimly. She'd lied to him. She'd betrayed him by not revealing her true self, her true nature. She'd walked out of his life eighteen months ago and he hadn't had enough of her. She'd left him aching and cursing her.

The fact that he'd once considered her suitable to be in his long-term future was a reminder that was unwelcome. This time when he took her he would know exactly who she was. And he would feel nothing but lust and desire. He would have her long legs wrapped around him again and he would sink deep enough inside her to burn away this irritating lingering lust.

He turned back to Rahul, who was looking nervous again.

'Sire, it was just a—'

Zafir cut him off. 'It was a brilliant suggestion and I know exactly who will be our model.'

Rahul frowned. 'Who, Sire?'

Zafir's pulse thundered in his veins. 'Kat Winters— the American supermodel. Find out where she is. Now.'

A week later, Queens, New York

Zafir observed her from the back of his car, with the window rolled down. He couldn't quite believe his eyes—that Kat Winters was working in a busy midrange restaurant in Queens. But, yes…one of the world's arguably most beautiful women was currently wearing skinny jeans and a white T-shirt with a black apron around her small waist. Her hair was piled up in a messy knot on her head and there was a pencil stuck through it, which she was now fumbling for as she took an order.

Everything in Zafir recoiled from this very banal scenario—except it wasn't disgust he was feeling, seeing her again. It was something much hotter and more urgent. Even dressed like this and without a scrap of make-up she was exquisite. A jewel such as she could not be hidden in a place like this. What the *hell* was she doing here? And what the hell was she doing going under another name—Kaycee Smith? And how dared she refuse to even consider the offer he'd sent to her via her agent?

Her agent had sent back a terse response:

Kat Winters is no longer available for modelling assignments.
Please do not pursue this request.

No one refused Zafir. Or warned him off. Least of all an ex-lover.

He issued a curt instruction to his driver now, and his window rolled up silently as he got out of the car and stretched to his full height of six foot four. He recalled Kat in vertiginous heels, the way it had put her mouth well within kissing distance. The way her added height had aligned their bodies so perfectly. He watched her walk away from the table and grimaced when he saw she was wearing sneakers.

Not for long, he vowed as he moved forward to the door of the restaurant. Soon she would be in heels again, and soon that lush mouth would be his again. All of her would be his again.

He had no idea what she was playing at, with this meek little game of being a waitress, but he was certain that once she heard what he had to say she'd be demonstrating her gratitude that he was prepared to give her another chance to be in his life and in his bed again, even just for a few brief weeks, in the most satisfactory way.

'Kat.'

It took a second for the significance of that word to sink in. No one here called her Kat. They called her Kaycee. And then there was the voice. Impossibly deep. And the way *Kat* had been pronounced, with the flat inflection that had always made it sound exotic. And authoritative—as if her name was a command to look at him, give him her attention.

It took another second for the realisation to hit her that there was only one person who could have spoken.

With the utmost reluctance, vying with disbelief, she looked up from the countertop.

Zafir.

For a moment she simply didn't believe it. He couldn't be here. Not against this very dull backdrop of a restaurant in Queens. He inhabited five-star zones. He breathed rarefied air. He moved in circles far removed from this place. This man was royalty.

He was a King now.

And yet her agent had told her only a couple of days ago that he'd asked for her, so she should have been prepared. But she'd blocked out any possibility of this happening. And now she was sorry, because she wasn't remotely prepared to see the man she'd loved with such intensity that it had sometimes scared her.

She blinked, but he didn't disappear. He seemed to grow in stature. Had he always been so tall? So broad? But she knew he had. He was imprinted on her brain and her memory like a brand. The hard-boned aristocratic features. The deep-set dark grey eyes that stood out against

his dark olive skin. The thick dark hair swept back off
his high forehead. That perfect hard-muscled body without an ounce of excess fat, its power evident even under
a suit and overcoat.

He was clean-shaven now, instead of with the short
beard he'd worn when she'd known him, and it should
have made him look somehow *less*. But it didn't. It
seemed to enhance his virility in a way that was almost
overwhelming.

She hadn't even realised she'd spoken his name out
loud until the sensual curve of those beautifully sculpted
lips curved up slightly on one side and he said, 'You remember my name, then?'

The mocking tone which implied that it was laughable
she could have possibly forgotten finally broke Kat out
of her dangerous reverie and shock. He *was* here. In her
space. The man she'd had dreams and nightmares about
meeting again now that her life had changed beyond all
recognition.

In her nightmares he looked at her with disgust and
horror, and to her mortification she woke up crying more
often than not. Her dreams were no less humiliating—
they were X-rated, and she'd wake up sweating, believing
for a second that she was still whole…still his.

But she was neither of those things. Not by a long shot.

Her pulse quickened treacherously, even though his
presence heralded an emotional pain she'd hoped had
been relegated to the past but which she was now dis-
covering not to be the case.

She spoke sharply. 'What are you doing here, Zafir?
Didn't you get my agent's message?'

He arched a brow and Kat flushed, suddenly aware of
how she'd just addressed a man before whom most people
would be genuflecting. A man who had two conspicuous
bodyguards dressed in black just outside the main door.

She refused to be intimidated. It was almost too much to take in, thinking of the last time she'd seen him and how upset she'd been, and then what had happened...the most catastrophic event of her life.

'I got her message and chose to ignore it,' Zafir said easily, his tone belying the curious punch to his gut when he registered Kat's obvious reluctance to see him again.

Kat folded her arms, as if that could protect her from his all too devastating charisma. Typical arrogant Zafir. He hadn't changed.

Tersely she said, 'I'm working, so unless you've come here to eat this isn't appropriate.' *It'll never be appropriate.* But she stopped herself from saying that with some desperation.

Zafir's smile faded and those unusual dark grey eyes flashed. 'You refused to engage with my offer, which I do not accept.'

'No,' Kat said, feeling the bitterness that was a residue from their last tumultuous meeting, when she'd left him. 'I can well imagine that you don't accept it, Zafir, because you're used to everyone falling over themselves to please you. But I'm afraid I feel no such compulsion.'

His eyes narrowed on her and she immediately felt threatened. She'd always felt as if he could see right through her—through the desperate façade she'd put up to try and convince people she wasn't a girl who had grown up in a trailer with a drug-addicted, mentally unstable mother. A girl who hadn't even graduated from high school.

Yet Zafir hadn't—for all that she'd thought he might. Until he'd had the evidence shoved under his nose and he'd looked at her with cold, unforgiving eyes and had judged and condemned her out of his life.

'You've changed.'

His words slammed into her like a physical blow. He

was right. She *had* changed. Utterly. And this was her worst nightmare coming to life. Meeting Zafir again. And him finding out—

He wouldn't, she assured herself now, feeling panicky. He couldn't.

'Is this gentleman looking for a table for one, Kaycee?'

Kat looked blankly at her boss for a second, but she didn't mistake the gleam of very feminine appreciation in the older woman's eyes as she ogled Zafir unashamedly.

Galvanised into action, she took the menu out of her boss's hands and said firmly, 'No, he's not. He was just looking for directions and now he knows where to go.' She looked at Zafir, and if she could have vaporised him on the spot she would have. 'Don't you, sir?'

Her boss was pulled aside at that moment by another member of staff, and Zafir just looked at Kat for a long moment, before saying silkily, 'I'll be waiting for you, *Kat*. This isn't over.'

And then he turned and walked out.

Kat really didn't want to leave the restaurant when her shift was over, because Zafir's car was still outside. As was the very conspicuous black four-by-four undoubtedly carrying his security team.

She was more than a little shocked that he was still waiting for her. Two hours later. The Zafir she'd known a year and a half ago had never waited for anyone—he'd been famously restless and impatient. Fools had suffered in his presence. He'd cut down anyone wasting his time with a glacial look from those pewter-coloured eyes.

As Kat dragged on her coat and belted it she felt a sense of fatalism settle over her. If Zafir had ignored her agent and tracked her down this far, then he wouldn't give up easily. She should know more than anyone that when he wanted something he pursued it until he got it.

After all, he'd pursued *her* until he'd got her. Until he'd dismantled every defence she'd erected to keep people from getting too close. Until she'd been prepared to give up everything for him. Until she'd been prepared to try and mould herself into what he'd wanted her to be—even though she'd known that she couldn't possibly fulfil everything he expected of her.

Her hands tightened on her belt for a moment. He'd asked her to be his Queen. Even now she felt the same mix of terror and awe at the very thought. But it hadn't taken much to persuade him of her unsuitability in the end.

She steeled herself before walking out through the door, telling herself that she was infinitely stronger now. Able to resist Zafir. He had no idea of what she'd faced since she'd seen him last...

As soon as she walked outside though, the back door of Zafir's sleek car opened and he emerged, uncoiling to his full impressive height. Kat's bravado felt very shaky all of a sudden.

He stood back and indicated with a hand for her to get in. Incensed that he might think it could be this easy, she walked over to him, mindful of her limp, even though disguising it after a long evening on her feet put pressure on her leg.

'I'm not getting into a car with you, Zafir. You've had a wasted evening. Please leave.'

She turned to walk away and she heard him say,

'Either we talk here on the sidewalk, with lots of ears about us, or you let me take you home and we talk there.'

Kat gritted her jaw and looked longingly down the street that would take her to her apartment, just a couple of blocks away. But if she walked away she could well imagine Zafir's very noticeable car moving at a snail's pace beside her. And his security team. Drawing lots of attention. As he was doing now, just by standing there, drawing lingering glances. Whispers.

A group of giggling girls finally made Kat turn around. 'Fine,' she bit out. 'But once I've listened to what you have to say you'll leave.'

Zafir's eyes gleamed in a way that made all the hard and cold parts of Kat feel dangerously soft and warm.

'By all means. If you want me to leave then, I'll leave.'

His tone once again told Kat that that was about as likely as a snowstorm in the middle of the brutally hot Jandor desert, and that only made her even more determined to resist him, hating that his visit was bringing up memories long buried. Memories of his beautiful and exotic country and how out of her depth she'd felt—both there and in their relationship. Zafir had been like the sun—brilliant, all-consuming and mesmerising, but fatal if one got too close. And she had let herself get too close. Close enough to be burnt alive once she'd discovered that the love she'd felt had been unrequited.

She'd been prepared to marry him, buoyed up by his proposal, only to discover too late that for him it had never been a romantic proposal. It had been purely because he'd deemed her 'perfect.' Her humiliation was still vivid.

She stalked past him now and got into the car, burningly aware of his gaze on her and wondering what on earth he must make of her—a shadow of her former self. The fact that she didn't seem to be repelling him irritated her intensely.

Zafir shut the door once her legs were in the car and came round and got in the other side, immediately dwarfing the expansive confines of the luxurious car. For a moment Kat felt herself sinking back into the seat, relishing the decadent luxury, but as soon as she realised what she was doing she stiffened against it. This wasn't her life any more. Never would be again.

'Kat?'

She looked at Zafir, who had a familiar expression of impatience on his face. She realised she hadn't heard what he'd said.

'Directions? For my driver?'

She swallowed, suddenly bombarded with a memory of being in the back of a very similar car with Zafir, when he'd asked his driver to put up the privacy window and drive around until he gave further instructions. Then he'd pulled Kat over to straddle his lap, pulled up her dress and—

She slammed the lid shut on that memory and leaned forward to tell the driver where to go before she lost her composure completely.

She refused to look at Zafir again, and within a couple of minutes they were pulling up outside her very modest apartment block. Kat managed to scramble inelegantly out of the car before Zafir could help her. She didn't want him to touch her—not even fleetingly. The thin threads holding her composure together might snap completely.

Her apartment was just inside the main doors of the apartment block, on the ground floor, and Kat could feel Zafir behind her. Tall, commanding. Totally incongruous.

As if to underline it she heard him say a little incredulously, 'No concierge?'

Kat would have bitten back a smile if she'd felt like smiling. 'No.'

She opened her door and went into her studio apartment. What had become a place of refuge for the past year was now anything but as she put her keys down and turned around to face her biggest threat.

Zafir closed the door behind him and Kat folded her arms. 'Well, Zafir? What is it you have to say?'

He was looking around the small space with unmistakable curiosity, and finally that dark grey gaze came to land on her. To her horror, he started to shrug off his overcoat, revealing a bespoke suit that clung lovingly to his powerful body.

When he spoke he sounded grim. 'I have plenty to say, Kat, so why don't you make us both a coffee? Because I'm not going anywhere any time soon.'

Kat stared mutinously at Zafir for a moment, and for those few seconds he was transfixed by her stunningly unusual eyes—amber from a distance, but actually green and gold from up close, surrounded by long dark lashes. They were almond-shaped, and Zafir's blood rushed south as he recalled how she'd look at him after making love, the expression in her gaze one of wonderment that had never failed to catch him like a punch to his gut.

Lies.

It had all been lies. She might have been a virgin, but she'd been no innocent. It had been an elaborate act to hide her murky past. Suddenly he felt exposed. What was he doing here?

But just then something in Kat's stance seemed to droop and she said in a resigned voice, 'Fine, I'll make coffee.'

She disappeared into a tiny galley kitchen and Zafir had to admit that he knew very well why he was here—he still wanted her. Even more so after seeing her again. But questions buzzed in his brain. He put down his overcoat on the back of a worn armchair and took in the clean but colourless furnishings of the tiny space she now called home.

He'd never been in the apartment she'd shared with three other models when he'd known her before, but it had been a loft in SoHo—a long way from here.

She emerged a couple of minutes later with two steaming cups and handed one to Zafir. He noticed that she was careful not to come too close, and it made something within him snarl and snap.

She'd taken off her coat and now wore a long-sleeved jumper over the T-shirt. Even her plain clothes couldn't hide that perfect body, though. High firm breasts. A small waist, generous hips. And legs that went on for ever...

He could still feel them, wrapped around his back, her heels digging into his buttocks as she urged him deeper, harder—

Dammit. He struggled to rein in his libido.

'Take a seat,' she said, with almost palpable reluctance.

Zafir took the opportunity to disguise his uncontrollable response, not welcoming it one bit. He put it down to his recent sexual drought.

She sat on a threadbare couch on the other side of a coffee table. Zafir took a sip of coffee, noting with some level of satisfaction that she hadn't forgotten how he liked it. Strong and black. But then he frowned, noticing something. 'Your hair is different.'

She touched a hand to the unruly knot on her head self-consciously. 'This is my natural colour.'

Zafir felt something inside him go cold when he observed that her 'natural colour' was a slightly darker brown, with enticing glints of copper. Wasn't this just more evidence of her duplicitous nature? Her hair had used to be a tawny golden colour, adding to her all-American, girl-next-door appeal, but in reality she'd made a mockery of that image.

He put down his cup. 'So, Kat, what happened? Why did you disappear off the international modelling scene and who is Kaycee Smith?'

CHAPTER TWO

ALL KAT HEARD WAS, 'Why did you disappear off the international modelling scene?' For a moment she couldn't breathe. The thought of letting exactly what had happened tumble out of her mouth and watching Zafir's reaction terrified her.

She'd come a long way in eighteen months, but some things she wasn't sure she'd ever be ready for...namely revealing to him the full reality of why she was no longer a model, or who she was now. The graceful long-legged stride she'd become famous for on catwalks all over the world was a distant memory now, never to be resurrected.

She breathed in shakily. *Answer his questions and then he'll be gone.* She couldn't imagine him wanting to hang around in these insalubrious surroundings for too long.

'What happened?' she said, in a carefully neutral voice. 'You know what happened, Zafir—after all you're the one who broke it to me that I'd been dropped from nearly every contract and that the fashion houses couldn't distance themselves fast enough from the girl who had fallen from grace.'

Kat had been blissfully unaware of the storm headed her way. She'd been packing for her new life with her fiancé—filled with trepidation, yes, but also hope that she would make him proud of her... What a naive fool she'd been.

Zafir's face darkened. 'There were *naked* pictures of you when you were seventeen years old, Kat. They spoke pretty eloquently for themselves. Not to mention the not inconsequential fact of the huge personal debt you'd been

hiding from me. And the real story of your upbringing—
enabling a drug-addicted mother to find her next fix.'

Kat's hands tightened on her cup as she remembered
the vicious headline Zafir had thrust under her nose.
It had labelled her 'a white trash gold-digger.' A man
like Zafir—privileged and richer than Croesus—could
never have begun to understand the challenges she'd faced
growing up.

Kat felt a surge of white-hot anger but also—far more
betrayingly—she felt hurt all over again. The fact that he
still had this ability to affect her almost killed her. Feeling too agitated to stay sitting, she put down her cup and
stood up, moving to stand behind the couch, as if that
could offer some scant protection.

Zafir was sitting forward, hands locked loosely between his legs. He looked perfectly at ease, but Kat wasn't
fooled by his stance. He was never more dangerous than
when he gave off an air of nonchalance.

'Look,' she said, as calmly as she could, 'if you've just
come here to re-enact our last meeting, then I can't see
how that will serve any purpose. I really don't need to be
reminded of how once my so-called perfect image was
tarnished you deemed me no longer acceptable in your
life. We said all we had to say that night.'

Her hands instinctively dug into the top of the couch
as she remembered that cataclysmic night—stumbling
out of Zafir's apartment building into the dark streets, the
pain of betrayal in her heart, her tear-blurred vision and
then... Nothing but blackness and more pain, the like of
which she hadn't known existed.

Zafir stood up too, dislodging the sickening memory,
reminding her that this was the present and apparently
not much had changed.

'Did we, really? As far as I recall you said far too little

and then left. You certainly didn't apologise for mislead-
ing me the whole time we were together.'

Struggling to control herself as she remembered the
awful shock of that night, Kat said, 'You saw that article
and you looked at those pictures and you judged and condemned me. You weren't prepared to listen to anything I
had to say in my defence.'

Kat's conscience pricked when she recalled how she'd
always put off telling Zafir the unvarnished truth of her
background. And as for the debt... She'd never wanted
to reveal that ugliness, or the awful powerlessness she'd
felt. Not to someone like Zafir, who set such an exacting
standard for moral strength and integrity.

'Dammit, Kat, you told me nothing about yourself—
when were you going to reveal the truth? If ever?' He
shook his head before she could respond, and repeated
his accusation of that night. 'You were obviously hoping that I'd marry you before the sordid details came out
and then you'd be secured for life even if we divorced.'

Kat felt breathless, and nausea rose inside her. 'It
wasn't like that...'

Zafir looked impossibly stern. As unforgiving as he
had been that night. He changed tack, asking her again,
'Who is Kaycee Smith?'

Kat swallowed painfully, not remotely prepared for
her past transgressions to be visited upon her again like
this. 'Kaycee Smith is the name on my birth certificate.'

A dark brow arched over one eye. 'A pertinent detail
missed by the papers?'

She refused to let Zafir do this to her again. Humili-
ate her. Annihilate her.

Kat tipped up her chin. 'It was about the only thing
they did miss.'

Thankfully, she thought now. Otherwise she would
never have been able to fade away from view as she had.

'We have nothing to say to each other, Zafir. *Nothing.* Now, get out—before I call the police and tell them you're harassing me.'

Kat moved decisively from her spot behind the sofa towards the door, powered by anger and the tumult inside her, only to be stopped in her tracks before she reached it when Zafir asked sharply, 'Why are you limping?'

Immediately the adrenalin rush faded, to be replaced with a very unwelcome sense of exposure. There was nothing to hold on to nearby and it reminded her of how vulnerable she was now.

She turned around slowly and realised that she was far too close to Zafir. Every part of her body seemed to hum with electricity. It was as if her libido had merely been waiting for his presence again, and now it was no longer dormant but very much awake and sizzling back to life.

His scent wound around her like a siren call to lean closer...to breathe in his uniquely male smell. It had always fascinated her—the mixture of earthy musk and something indescribably exotic which instantly brought her back to her first and last visit to Jahor, with its awe-inspiring palace on a hill overlooking the teeming ancient city on the edge of the ocean.

She'd felt so awed and intimidated at the prospect of becoming a Queen of that land, and yet deep within her she'd thrilled to the challenge. But when Zafir had deemed her unsuitable to be his wife she'd realised what a fool she'd been to indulge in such a fantasy. She was no Queen, and she had no right to the ache of loss that still had the power to surprise her when she wasn't vigilant.

Her head snapped up. Zafir was still frowning. She moved back, aghast that her body could betray her like this. And then she remembered what he'd asked: *Why are you limping?*

Everything inside Kat recoiled from revealing herself to Zafir. The urge to self-protect was huge. He had no idea of the extent of the devastation in her life since she'd seen him—not all of which had to do with him. It also had to do with events totally beyond him.

But she knew that giving him nothing would only pique his interest even more, so reluctantly she said, 'I was involved in a road traffic accident a while ago. I injured my leg and I was out of circulation for some time.'

Try at least a year, Kat thought to herself, and held her breath, praying he wouldn't ask for more details.

Zafir looked at her assessingly. 'Is that why you haven't returned to modelling? And is that why you're living like this? Because you still haven't cleared your debts? You're obviously recovered now though, and I can't imagine the fashion world wouldn't have renewed your contracts eventually, once the story had died down.'

Kat hid her reflexive flinch at *'you're obviously recovered now.'* But she wasn't about to explain anything—not when Zafir was clearly no more ready to hear the truth now than he had been back then. And he was right—except when the fashion houses *had* come calling again she'd been in no position to consider going back…

Kat breathed out unsteadily. She avoided answering his questions directly and said, 'I do some hand modelling, but that's about it. And the waitressing.'

Zafir came closer, standing beside the chair. His gaze was far too keen on her and incisive. She could almost hear his brain working, trying to join the dots.

Kat just wanted him gone. He'd upended her world once before and she wouldn't survive him doing it again.

'Look,' she said now, trying to hide the desperation in her voice, 'did you really come here to rake over old ground, Zafir?'

She stopped and bit her lip as a dangerous thought

occurred to her—perhaps in spite of everything he *had* come to listen to her side of the story? Even belatedly?

For a moment Kat felt something very delicate flower deep inside her, but after a moment Zafir shook his head and said curtly, 'No. Of course not. That's in the past and I've no wish to revisit it any further.'

Kat's heart thumped. Hard. Of course he hadn't come here to hear her side of things. Apparently she was as pathetically susceptible to this man as she'd ever been, and in spite of everything she'd been through that was somehow more devastating than anything else. She felt a dart of panic at the knowledge that time had done little to diminish her feelings or her attraction to him. If anything, everything felt more acute than it had before.

She forced out words through a tight jaw. 'Then if you wouldn't mind leaving? We had a past and you pretty definitively ruled out any future, so what more could there possibly be to say?'

She regretted asking the question as soon as she saw the calculating gleam come into those slate-grey eyes.

'Our future is exactly what I'm here to talk about. A different future to the one previously envisaged, yes, but I don't see why we can't leave that in the past and move on.'

Kat's insides tightened as if warding off a blow. 'I'm not interested in discussing any kind of future or *moving on* with you, Zafir.'

Zafir's jaw clenched and he had to consciously relax it. He wasn't used to anyone talking to him like this—and he couldn't remember Kat ever being so combative. But he couldn't deny that somewhere deep inside him he thrilled to it. She *had* changed, and yet she was still intriguingly familiar. Achingly familiar. His whole body hummed with frustration to be so close and yet have her hold him at arm's length and look at him as if he was an unwelcome stranger.

In truth, he hadn't expected her to be so antagonistic towards him. He knew things had ended badly before, but she was the one who had kept the truth from him, clearly in a bid to avoid risking his commitment to marry her—which was exactly what had happened. Yet she was acting as if she was the injured party!

He cursed himself. He hadn't planned on rehashing the past, but obviously it had been inevitable. But, as he'd said, he was done talking about the past now—it was time for him to lay out his plans for Kat. For *them*.

In spite of everything, and even though he knew there were a thousand reasons for him to turn and walk away from Kat and forget he'd ever seen her again, he *couldn't*. Not now. But he assured himself that he could have what he wanted and get on with his life. And he fully intended to.

'I'm not leaving until I've said what I came to say, Kat.'

Dismayed, Kat watched as Zafir illustrated his point by sitting down again. He was an immovable force, and she recognised that steely determination all too well. The last thing she wanted was for him to see how raw she felt, so she schooled her features and sat down opposite him, as if this visit wasn't tearing her apart.

She looked pointedly at her watch and then back to him, 'It's getting late and I've got work early in the morning. I'd appreciate it if you could keep this short.'

Zafir inspected the bland expression on Kat's face. For a moment he'd caught a glimpse of something much more fiery, but it was gone now. She seemed to be determined to treat him as if he was someone she hadn't been intimately acquainted with. Soon, Zafir vowed, they would be intimately acquainted again, and she'd be moaning his name in ecstasy as her release threw them both over the edge and purged him of this ache.

He forced his mind out of his fantasies with effort and said, 'Did you even listen to the proposition I sent your agent?'

Kat shook her head, a long tendril of hair dropping from the knot on top of her head to curl around her neck. Zafir wanted to undo her hair and let it fall in a luxurious curtain down her naked back, the way it had before. He gritted his jaw at the image. This was ridiculous—he could barely conduct a coherent conversation without X-rated images flooding his mind.

Calling on every ounce of control he possessed, he said, 'What I'm proposing is a modelling assignment—'

He stopped and put up his hand as soon as he saw Kat's mouth open, presumably to protest. She closed it again, her lush lips compressing into a tight line. Zafir ignored the pulse throbbing in his groin.

He tried another tack. 'You might recall me telling you once about the famed missing jewel, the Heart of Jandor, the biggest red diamond in the world?'

Kat tensed opposite him, and then he saw a flush tinge her cheeks pink as if she too was remembering that moment—lying in her bed in Jahor, her limbs sprawled over his in sated abandon as he'd told her the story of the gem. He'd had to sneak into her rooms like a teenager, even though they'd been unofficially engaged at the time. His people would have been scandalised by such liaisons.

Kat had lifted her head from his chest and said huskily, 'That's so romantic… I hope they find it some day.'

Zafir could recall how a vague feeling of dread mixed with fear had washed over him on hearing the wistful tone in Kat's voice, and how he'd felt the urge to say something, *anything*, to take the dreamy look from her eyes, to tell her that such a thing as romance had no place in his life. Duty trumped emotion. Always. There would be no room for romance when he became King and she was Queen.

But then she'd reached up and kissed him...and he couldn't remember anything else.

'I remember something...vaguely,' she said tightly now, and Zafir desisted from arguing that she clearly remembered very well.

There was a curt edge to his voice after that memory. 'They found the diamond recently, during an archaeological dig. It was a cause of much celebration and my people have seen it as a good omen for the future.'

Kat's hands were clasped in her lap. 'I'm very happy for you...and them...but I fail to see what this has to do with me.'

Zafir said carefully, 'It has everything to do with you, Kat, because I've chosen you to be the model who will wear the diamond on our worldwide diplomatic tour to promote Jandor.'

The sheer arrogance of Zafir's pronouncement rendered Kat speechless for a moment. And then she spluttered, 'But that's ridiculous. I'm working here. I have a life here. I have no intention of going anywhere with you.'

Zafir stood up, and as if she hadn't spoken he said, 'It's a very select tour. The first function is the evening after tomorrow, at the Metropolitan Museum of Art. Then we and the diamond go to London, then Paris and then back to Jandor, where it will be put on permanent display.'

Kat stood up, quivering all over with volatile emotions. 'There is no *we* in this, Zafir.'

'If it had gone according to my plan, then, yes, I agree—I would have no need of you. But my chief aide came up with the idea of showing off the diamond in an infinitely more accessible way—instead of keeping it in a sterile environment, we will display it on a beautiful woman and have her meet and greet specially selected guests with us at each function, so that they can see how the gem really glows with a life force. It will bring the gem—and Jandor—alive.'

Kat folded her arms against the terrifying thought of people clamouring around her, too close, staring at her, pawing at her to get to the stone. One of the side effects of the accident she'd been involved in was that she felt claustrophobic in certain situations where she felt trapped.

She shook her head. 'No way, Zafir. I'm not interested. And surely if this is to promote your country, then you should be using a model from Jandor.'

Kat saw the steely glint in Zafir's eyes. It meant that he'd most likely anticipated every one of her arguments and was ready to counter them.

'We don't yet have a modelling agency in Jandor, but we *do* have aspiring fashion designers who are eager to showcase some of their designs during this tour. Also, I want someone who has the poise and grace of an experienced model—and they don't come more experienced than you.'

Feeling desperate, she said, 'There are a million models just as experienced as me—if not more.' A hint of bitterness crept into her voice. 'Models who don't come with negative baggage. If I appear in public with you as Kat Winters, the press will have a field day and all those stories will get raked up again.'

Kat sent up silent thanks now that their break-up had occurred before the official public announcement of their engagement had been made.

'Yes, they might,' he conceded, 'and I've considered that. But I have an excellent PR team, who will field any of the old stories and drown them out with this new one.

Resurrecting Kat Winters to wear the most famous re-discovered gem in the world will be an irresistible story.'

Kat went cold inside as the full extent of Zafir's cool calculation sank in. Her involvement would be purely to provide an angle. Something to fire up the headlines even at the expense of negativity. Everything Zafir was outlining was literally her worst nightmare. She felt pan-icky. She wasn't prepared to step back into the world of Kat Winters again—not for anyone.

She shook her head. 'The answer is no, Zafir. Now, please leave. I'm tired.'

But of course Zafir didn't turn around to leave, much as Kat wished he would. Even as she felt the betraying hum of awareness that flowed like illicit nectar through her blood.

'Obviously I wouldn't expect you to do this for free, Kat. I would be willing to pay handsomely for one of the world's most sought-after and elusive models. I'm well aware of the fees you once commanded, and as your credit history shows a lack of ability to hang on to your earnings, it looks like you're not really in a position to turn down such a lucrative contract.'

He illustrated his point with a sweeping glance around her studio apartment.

Kat's hands curled into fists. *Of all the patronising—* She stopped just as she was about to blurt something out. Something that would make those far too incisive eyes narrow on her and make him start asking questions again.

It was the last thing she wanted to bring up, but she had to. Maybe it was the thing that would finally push Zafir to leave. 'Have you considered the speculation that would inevitably be sparked about *us* again?'

He waited a beat and then said, 'Yes, I have, and I see no harm in it—not when it's likely to be confined to the duration of the tour and then it'll die away again.'

There was a rough quality to Zafir's voice that sent a rush of awareness through Kat's blood—as if her body was already reacting to some secret signal. For a moment she couldn't really comprehend the way he was suddenly so watchful, but then it sank in with horrifying clarity.

'You can't seriously mean for us to—' She stopped, afraid to speak the words out loud. Afraid to make herself look a fool again. Afraid she might be right.

Afraid she might be wrong.

'Can't seriously mean for us to what, Kat?'

Zafir moved closer and she was rooted to the spot. He stopped within reaching distance, the harsh lighting of her apartment doing nothing to leach away any of his sheer gorgeousness.

'I can't seriously mean for us to be together again?'

Kat looked at him, horrified and excited in equal measure. She half shook and nodded her head.

Zafir's face suddenly took on a harsh aspect. 'That's exactly what I mean. I want you back in my bed, Kat. We have unfinished business. When you walked out—'

'You mean when you cast me aside!' Anger flooded Kat's veins again, giving her the impetus to move back out of Zafir's dangerous proximity, crossing her arms defensively over her chest.

'We're not going to rake over that ground again,' Zafir said harshly. 'Suffice it to say that our engagement might have been over—there was no way I could have presented you as my future Queen after those headlines and pictures—but our relationship didn't have to be over.'

Shock mixed with affront, and hurt poured through Kat, making her tremble. She was back in time, standing before Zafir in far more luxurious surroundings saying incredulously, 'You don't love me.'

He'd slashed a hand through the air. 'This isn't about *love*, Kat. It's never been about love. It's about mutual

respect and desire and the fact that I believed—mistak-
enly—that you were the perfect choice to be my wife
and future Queen.'

'*Perfect...*' She'd half-whispered it to herself, never
hating a word as much as she had then.

Her whole life she'd been told she had to be *perfect*.
To win the next competition. To get the commercial over
the other pretty girl. To get enough money to save her
mother... Except she'd failed—miserably.

She'd looked at Zafir and said in a hollow voice, 'Well,
I'm not perfect, Zafir. Far from it.'

And she'd walked out, leaving her engagement ring on
the hall table. And now she was glad—because clearly
he would have demoted her from the position of future
wife, but kept her in his life as his mistress.

And she'd never been further from perfect than she
was right now.

'Get out, Zafir, this conversation is over.'

But her words bounced off him as if an invisible shield
protected him.

'Think about what you're turning down, Kat. A chance
to restart your life and return to where you belong. Have
you thought about what you'd be turning down?'

He mentioned a sum of money and it was literally life-
changing. Kat felt her blood drain south.

He reached into an inside pocket and took out a card,
holding it out to her. She unlocked her arms from her
chest and took it reluctantly.

'That's my private number. I'll be staying at my penthouse apartment. I'll give you till tomorrow morning,
Kat. If I don't hear from you I *will* find someone else and
you will never hear from me again.'

She looked at him and marvelled that she'd once believed that he loved her because he'd asked her to marry
him. Because she'd always had a romantic notion that that

was what people did when they loved someone, in spite of being brought up as the only child of a single parent with no clue as to her father's whereabouts.

But Zafir's motives had been so much more strategic than that. She'd been scrutinised and deemed suitable. *Perfect.* And now he was asking her to step back into a world that had chewed her up and spat her out. Not only that, he was asking her to lay herself bare to him again, to let him carve out the last remaining part of her heart that still functioned and let him crush it until there was nothing left.

Kat was stronger now than she'd ever been, considering the trials she'd faced in the past eighteen months, but she was still only human and she wasn't strong enough for this. No matter how much money he was offering.

Without taking her eyes off Zafir's, as if some small, treacherous part of her wanted to commit them to her memory, she held up the card and ripped it in half, letting the pieces fall to the floor.

'Goodbye, Zafir.'

His eyes flashed and his jaw clenched. Kat could feel the waves of energy flowing like electricity between them, but after a tense moment he just stepped back and said, 'As you wish. Goodbye, Kat.'

But to Kat's dismay, when Zafir finally turned and walked out, picking up his overcoat as he did so, and when the door had shut behind him, the last thing she felt was triumph.

She found her feet moving towards the door instinctively, as if to rush after him and beg him not to go. She stopped in her tracks, shocked at the profound sense of loss that pervaded her whole body, and she wrapped her arms around herself as if that could hold back all the turmoil she was feeling.

Zafir had devastated her once before. She couldn't let it happen again.

So she stayed resolutely where she was, and after she'd heard the sound of his vehicles leaving from outside the apartment she breathed in shakily and sank down onto the couch behind her.

She looked around her, as if seeing the space for the first time again. She'd grown used to the bare furnishings and the sparse décor. It was all she'd been able to afford after the accident and her lengthy rehabilitation, even though the largest part of her debt had finally been gone.

And the reason it had been gone was because once those pictures of Kat had gone public, her blackmailer—the photographer who had taken them in the first place—had had no further means with which to blackmail her. After all, everything he'd always threatened her with had come true—her career had imploded in spectacular style.

Perversely, Kat had been grateful to whoever had found and leaked the pictures, because they had freed her from a malignant threat she'd had no idea how to deal with.

On numerous occasions she'd wanted to confide in Zafir, but then she'd feel too intimidated, or too scared of his reaction. How could a man like him, who had grown up in such a rarefied world, possibly understand why she would do such a thing? The thought of revealing all that ugly poison had pulled her back from the brink each time.

And in the end hadn't she been vindicated? She'd never forget the look of disgust and horror on his face as he'd confronted her with her past.

Kat stood up again, restless, as Zafir's visit sank in properly. She told herself that it was his arrogance that still left her breathless, but really it was the knowledge that he still wanted her, and the even more shattering knowledge that she still wanted him. The core of her body felt hot and achy, and her blood felt thick and heavy in her veins.

Damn him.

She paced back and forth, and as she did so her eye snagged on something in the corner of the room and she stopped. Zafir hadn't noticed them. Crutches and a folded-up wheelchair. She hadn't needed the wheelchair for some time now, but she would never *not* need one to hand. And she'd always need the crutches.

To Kat's shame, she knew that *this* was as much of a reason as any other as to why she'd all but pushed Zafir out through the door. Because she couldn't bear for him to know what had happened to her. Because she couldn't bear to think about the fact that, even if she *was* to ever be with Zafir again, he would not want to be with her.

Because she was irrevocably altered.

Kat picked up the crutches and went into her tiny bedroom. She took off her sneakers, undid her jeans and pulled them off, then stood in front of her mirror, inspecting herself critically.

At first glance Zafir might not notice anything different about Kat—after all she stood on two legs, and was the same height she'd always been, with the same straight back. But then she imagined his gaze travelling down and stopping on her left leg. Specifically on the prosthetic limb that now made up her lower left leg, with its mechanical ankle and fake foot.

Even now Kat couldn't recall anything about the accident itself on that fateful night. She only knew that one minute she'd been crossing the street and the next she'd been waking up, a day later, in a hospital, with a doctor informing her that they'd had to amputate below the knee to save her leg—which was kind of ironic, considering half of it was now gone.

She'd had flashbacks however, since then, of regaining consciousness and realising that her foot was trapped under the heaviest weight. People had crowded around her but she hadn't been able to move or speak. And then she'd slipped back into darkness.

That was why she got claustrophobic now.

Sometimes people gave her a second glance, but they soon dismissed her when they saw her slightly limping gait and figured this woman with darker hair and no make-up couldn't possibly be *the* Kat Winters.

A ball of emotion lodged itself in Kat's chest, and before she could stop them hot tears blurred her vision. But she dashed them away angrily as she sat down on her bed and set about removing her prosthetic limb with an efficiency born of habit.

It had been a long time since she'd indulged in self-pity. That had been in the dark early days, when she'd fallen down in many graceless heaps while trying to get to the bathroom during the night, when she'd hurled her crutches across the room in a rising tide of fury at the hand she'd been dealt. Or when she'd locked herself away for long days, sunk in such a black depression that she'd thought she might never emerge into daylight again.

It was her oldest friend, Julie, who was also her agent, who had finally saved her. And the local rehabilitation centre. It was there that she'd learnt how to deal with her new reality and had been able to start putting things into perspective after meeting a man who had lost both his legs in a war, and a woman who had lost an arm, and an endlessly cheerful little girl who'd lost her limbs after meningitis... They, and many more, had humbled her, and reminded her that she was one of the luckier ones.

And gradually she'd clawed her way out of the mire to a place of acceptance, where this was her new reality and she just had to get on with it. And she *had* been getting on with it, perfectly well, until a Zafir-shaped storm had blown everything up again.

Kat could be honest enough with herself to acknowledge that—as much as the accident and its consequences had made her feel as if her life had shrunk—she'd been living in a kind of limbo, taking one day at a time. The accident had been so catastrophic that she'd been able to block out that last night with Zafir for a long time, but recently it had been creeping back, as if now she was ready to deal with it...

Maybe he was right, whispered a coaxing voice. *Maybe you do have unfinished business. Perhaps if you took on the assignment you could lay more than one ghost to rest.*

The ghost of the relationship she'd *thought* she had with Zafir, but which had never really existed...only in her romantic fantasies.

The ghost of the Kat Winters she'd been before—in awe and intimidated by nearly everything and everyone around her in spite of her high-flying career, and by none more so than Sheikh Zafir Ibn Hafiz Al-Noury. The ghost of her mother's death and the constant feeling of failure Kat had grown up with when she hadn't been able to save a mother who hadn't wanted to be saved.

The thought lodged in Kat's head, and as much as she wanted to dismiss it out of hand she was afraid that she couldn't go back to fooling herself that Zafir was firmly in her past. She'd been too scared to really look at the repercussions of what had happened between them, but seeing him again this evening had roused more than one dormant part of her.

Not least of which was the reawakening of her sexual awareness. It was terrifying. The prospect of intimacy and what it would mean now was something she'd found easy to bury deep inside her since the accident. If she'd thought about it at all, she'd imagined that it would be with someone gentle, kind...patient.

Zafir was a force of nature—above such benign human virtues. He didn't have to deal with imperfection. He walked amongst the brightest, the best, the most beautiful. He was one of them.

Panic skittered up Kat's spine. There was no way she felt ready to trust Zafir on an intimate level again with her *new* self.

Resolutely shutting her mind to that scenario, she thought again of that fateful night and their fight.

Her conscience pricked when she remembered rushing out of his apartment—had she been too hasty? But once she'd known that he didn't love her, the last thing she'd wanted to do was try to defend herself to someone who had only ever seen her as some kind of a commodity.

That's how her mother had seen her—as a means to make money, capitalising on her daughter's beauty. Zafir had been no different—he'd all but admitted he'd only proposed because she'd fitted into his life on a superficial level and nothing more. It had driven home to Kat how much she hungered to be loved for her whole self.

But she had the sinking feeling that her secret wounds would remain raw until she confronted Zafir properly and forced him to listen to her side of the story behind those lurid headlines.

Not that she wanted anything more than that... The prospect of *more* made panic surge again even as her blood grew hot.

She would deny that her attraction to him was as strong as ever with every breath in her body—she had no intention of ever letting Zafir see her like this. She looked down at her residual limb and ran a hand over it almost protectively.

Yet even as she entertained the possibility of acqui-

escing to his demand—purely on a professional basis—
she balked at the thought. The prospect of going back
into that world and being scrutinised terrified her. And
doing it all with Zafir by her side? Scrambling her brain
to pieces? Making all the cold parts of her melt again
after she'd spent so much time rebuilding her defences?

No way. She couldn't. She wasn't strong enough yet.

At that moment Kat caught sight of her reflection in
the mirror as she sat on the bed. Her eyes were huge. She
looked panicked and pale… Something inside her resisted that. She sat up straight and took in the full reality
of who she was now. A damaged woman, yes, and less
whole than she'd once been, but actually in many ways
more whole than she'd ever been.

She'd always known on some level that she wasn't prepared to hide away as Kaycee Smith for ever, and Julie
had been putting more and more pressure on her to come
out of her protective cocoon, to let herself be seen again.

And now Zafir was asking her to take on a modelling assignment. That was all. *No, it's not,* whispered a
snide voice, and Kat's heart thumped in response. Zafir
had wanted perfection before, and he'd rejected her because she'd fallen from grace. She would never give him
a chance to do that to her again.

She thought of the sum of money he'd mentioned and
realised with a churning gut that it would allow her to pay
Julie back. Her friend had helped support Kat through
not only the first six months of her rehabilitation, but
since then too, because Kat had only had the most basic
of insurance. But also—and maybe more important—
she realised that she would be able to help the rehabilitation centre that had been so instrumental in her recovery.

The St Patrick's Medical Centre for Traumatic Inju-
ries was currently facing the prospect of closure due to
lack of funds and resources. Kat would be in a position to

give them enough money to avoid imminent closure until they could get back on their feet and raise more funds for their long-term future.

If she accepted Zafir's job offer.

Her heart sped up with a mixture of terror and illicit excitement—if she said yes, then she could use it as an exercise to prove to herself just how ill-suited she and Zafir had always been, in spite of the insane chemistry between them. Never more evident than now. She was no longer a wide-eyed virgin being initiated into a world that had moved at a terrifying pace—too fast for her to shout, *'Stop!'* and get off.

She was strong enough to take on Zafir and walk away with her head high.

Are you really, though?

Kat assured herself that, yes, she was.

This would be purely a professional transaction. Zafir would never touch her emotions again—or her body. He was the kind of man who relished the conquest, who relished making a woman acquiesce to him of her own volition, and she had no intention of acquiescing to an affair.

The walls Kat had had to build just to survive since the accident were impenetrable. He wouldn't break through. She could do this.

She picked up her mobile from the table near the bed before she lost her nerve, focusing on anything but the terror she felt at the thought of what she was about to do. And how it would affect her life.

This wasn't just about her. Not when she now knew she could put that money to good use. Vital use.

Zafir had made it clear that he would walk away, and if Kat knew anything about him it was that he meant what he said. He was a proud man. He wouldn't ask again and he certainly wouldn't beg.

As Kat dialled her friend's number and waited for her

to answer, she caught sight of her reflection in the mirror again. She scowled at her flushed face and the too-bright eyes that whispered that her decision had a lot less to do with altruism and more to do with something much darker and far more ambiguous deep inside her.

And then Julie answered and Kat had a split second to decide whether to take a step into a dangerous future or remain safe in the past.

CHAPTER THREE

ZAFIR STOOD AT the window of his penthouse study and looked out over Manhattan, sparkling under the autumn sun, with Central Park in the distance. He was trying not to acknowledge the sense of triumph and satisfaction rushing through his blood, but it was hard.

Along with it, though, had come something far more contradictory—a kind of disappointment—and Zafir realised that it was because when he'd walked away from Kat last night she'd seemed so resolute. And, as much as it had irritated him intensely, he'd admired it on some level. It was rare to find anyone going against him in anything—especially since he'd become King.

He recalled getting into his car last night and how stunned he'd been that she'd turned him down. And then how he'd had to physically restrain himself from instructing his driver to turn around so that he could go back to Kat's apartment and shatter that cooler than cool reception by reminding her in a very explicit way of just how good it had been between them. How good it could be again.

And yet before 8:00 a.m. this morning his personal phone had rung and it had been her agent, confirming that Kat had decided to take on the assignment after all.

At this very moment she was with her agent and his legal advisors, signing the contract, and then she was due to spend the rest of the day and tomorrow in preparation for the tour with a team of stylists. Rahul would go through the itinerary with her and make sure her passport and travel documents were in order for when they left the United States.

So her cold stonewalling and reluctance last night had been an act. Much like the act she'd fooled everyone with when he'd first met her, projecting a false persona of someone who was honest and hard-working, making the most of the opportunities presented to her.

She'd been honest, at least, about coming from a poor background—which in Zafir's eyes had only made her more commendable. She'd epitomised the American dream of grit and ambition and achieving success no matter what your circumstances were.

But in actual fact her story had been a lot darker and murkier. She'd had a huge personal debt she'd never revealed—in spite of commanding eye-wateringly high fees as one of the most in-demand models of her time. She'd had a drug-addicted mother, no father to speak of, and barely any education. Not to mention the coup de grâce— those provocative pictures taken when she was only seventeen years old, apparently in a bid to make money so her mother could score her next fix.

Even now when Zafir thought of those explicit pictures he felt his vision cloud over with a red mist and his hands curl to fists in his pockets. Kat had been so young, and yet she'd looked at the camera almost defiantly. The rage he'd felt towards the person behind the camera had scared him with its intensity. But what he'd felt towards Kat had been much more complicated—anger, disappointment. Protectiveness. *Betrayal.*

When he'd confronted her with the headlines due to hit the news stands within hours, he'd wanted to hear her say that she'd been an unwilling victim, so that he could apportion blame to someone else and not her... But she'd agreed with him that she was not perfect. That she was flawed. And then she'd walked out of his apartment and disappeared, leaving him with a futile anger that had corroded his insides as he'd gone over it in his head again and again, trying to make sense of how he could have been so naive...

It had made him doubt if she'd even been a virgin, or if that had been part of an elaborate ruse to attract his jaded interest. Certainly her innocence had shocked him at the time when she'd admitted it; he'd believed virgins in their twenties to be as mythical as unicorns, and it had dissolved some of Zafir's very cynical defences.

And yet in spite of that history he was bringing her back into his world. *Because he had to have her.* Zafir's jaw clenched. He did not like being at the mercy of desires he couldn't control. Maybe it had something to do with the fact that he'd been her first lover, making his connection to her feel somehow more primal...

But, he reasoned to himself, now he knew all Kat's secrets. Now he knew that she was suitable only to sate this fever burning in his body. He would never put her on a pedestal again, or imagine for a second that she could be the woman who would stand alongside him in front of his people.

Kat took in her reflection in the floor-length mirror. At that moment she was almost glad that Julie had had to leave her with the team of stylists and hair and make-up artists and go back to work. She needed to be alone right now.

She was dressed from head to toe in a black velvet sleeveless haute couture gown with a deep vee that ran almost down to her navel, exposing more skin than she had in years. Her hair was pulled back in a rough chignon. The heavy make-up felt strange on her face after not wearing any for so long. And she was wearing heels—albeit only two-inch heels.

Her critical gaze travelled down her body and she lifted up the bottom of the dress. Her breath caught. To the untrained eye her legs looked absolutely normal. As they'd always looked.

In the place of her habitual prosthetic limb was the cosmetic one that Julie had insisted on Kat being fitted for some months ago. It had been specially made for her in a factory in the UK, in a bid to show Kat that perhaps embarking on more than hand modelling was possible, but this was the first time she'd put it to use. And luckily the fit was still fine.

Kat looked down. It was remarkable. Her toenails were painted. She could even see veins. No one would notice a thing. A bubble of emotion rose up from her chest and she looked up again, letting the dress fall back, blinking her eyes rapidly to get rid of the sudden and mortifying onset of tears.

She was slightly ashamed of how overcome she felt to see herself like this, when she'd never expected to see herself like this again. When she'd thought she'd closed the door firmly on her old life. When she'd told herself that she'd never *really* felt a part of that world.

And yet here she was, feeling such a mix of emotions that it only proved to her that she was more tied to her old life than she'd realised.

A sharp rap sounded on the door to the bedroom in the lavish suite where she'd been changing into countless outfits and she called out hurriedly, 'Just a second.'

No doubt the stylists were eager to see the dress on her, as it was the one she'd wear on the first night of the tour, chosen for its clean lines so that the diamond would be shown to its best advantage.

She composed herself and held the dress to her chest where it was still a little loose. As she opened the door she said, 'The fit is fine. I just need to be zipped—'

The words died on her tongue and she had to look up and up again at the man filling the doorway. *Zafir.* She hadn't seen him when they'd arrived earlier to sign the contract, and she'd felt jittery with nerves, waiting for him to appear at any moment. When he hadn't, she'd almost fooled herself into thinking that this assignment was not at his behest.

But it was. And here he was, wearing a shirt and dark trousers, his top button open and sleeves rolled up. She guessed that he'd just come from his office. He always had been a workaholic.

He was as leanly muscled as she remembered, the power in his body evident in a provocatively subtle way that was mesmerising and made her think of how he'd looked in his traditional Jandori robes—like a fierce warrior.

His voice broke her out of her embarrassing trance. 'You'd like me to zip you up?'

Anyone but you.

Kat clutched the dress to her breasts even more tightly, suddenly feeling as shy as the virgin she'd once been, in front of him.

She tried to look past him. 'I can ask one of the stylists…' Then she realised how quiet it was. 'Where is everyone?'

'I sent them away for the evening.' Zafir looked at his watch. 'It's 4:30 p.m. They've been working all day and so have you.'

Kat looked at him a little stupidly. She hadn't even realised how late it had got.

He lifted his hands. 'The dress? I'd like to see how it looks with the diamond.'

Kat balked. 'You have it with you now?'

Zafir nodded.

With the utmost reluctance Kat moved closer and turned around, presenting her bare back to him. She'd never before realised how vulnerable it felt—exposing the most defenceless part of your body to someone you didn't trust.

Yet even as she told herself that she didn't trust him she had to suppress the betraying shiver of anticipation that ran through her body as she waited for Zafir to pull up the zip. It didn't help when countless memories bombarded her of similar moments, when he had pressed close behind her and moved his hands around and under her dress to cup her breasts, pressing a hot kiss to her neck.

She hadn't felt vulnerable or defenceless then. Far from it.

She'd trusted him.

Her nerves were jangling painfully when she finally felt his hands on the zip, just above her buttocks, and then its far too slow ascent up her back, pulling the dress tighter around her torso, so that her breasts were pushed together under the discreet boning, creating a voluptuous cleavage. Something that wouldn't have bothered her too much in the past, but which felt positively indecent now.

When the zip was up she quickly turned around and moved out of touching distance. Zafir's eyes were a dark grey. To her relief he moved back and stood aside so she could walk out of the bedroom and into the suite. The unsteadiness of her legs had nothing to do with her prosthetic limb.

Kat stopped in her tracks, though, when a young woman dressed in a sober black suit, with her dark hair pulled back, stepped out of the shadows to stand beside the table where a large black box sat.

She'd thought they were alone, but they weren't. Perversely, that didn't seem to be of any comfort.

Zafir walked over to the table with his innately masculine grace, saying as he did so, 'I'd like you to meet Noor Qureshi. She's going to be your personal bodyguard for the duration of the tour while you wear the diamond.'

Kat put out her hand, slightly in awe of the female bodyguard. 'It's nice to meet you.'

They shook hands, but Zafir was drawing Kat's attention to the box, where he had his hand on the open lid. Kat came forward as Zafir said something to Noor, and the woman nodded before slipping discreetly out of the main suite door, presumably to wait outside.

Kat barely noticed. She fancied she could almost see the red-hued glow before she saw the actual diamond, and when she stepped close enough to see the stone resting against the black silk she gasped.

It was literally breathtaking. A stone about the size of a golf ball, in a heart shape. It seemed to glow and emit some kind of luminosity. Kat could imagine how it must have appeared when it was first discovered, deep in the mines, even in its rough state.

Zafir lifted it out and Kat saw that the gem sat in a thick collar-style platinum setting, and that the platinum was inscribed with what looked like Arabic script. The diamond dropped from the collar, stark and hypnotic.

Zafir held the necklace up, clearly indicating that he wanted to put it on Kat, and once again she stood in front of him, and shivered slightly as his arms came around her and the red diamond necklace appeared in her eye-line. She could feel him behind her, the heat and strength of his body.

It was one of the things that had drawn her to him like a helpless moth to a bright burning flame. His very masculinity. And it had surprised her, because ever since she'd been tiny she'd been aware of men and their strength, and how they could use it against a woman, after witnessing her mother bringing home one abusive male after another.

But Zafir was the first physically powerful man who had connected with Kat on another level and she hadn't instinctively shied away from him. To the contrary. And now she was feeling that same pull—as if her body was a magnet, aligned only to his and no one else's.

She closed her eyes for a second, as if that would help fight his pull, and then she felt the weight of the stone land on her upper chest. It was warm, not cold, and she instinctively reached up to touch it, feeling the pointed end. The metal of the collar was cool where it touched her skin.

Zafir's fingers brushed the back of her neck as he closed the clasp and then they were gone, and the necklace felt heavy around Kat's neck. He came and stood in front of her, looking at the stone and then at her, critically.

'Move back,' he commanded.

Kat felt an urge to resist his autocratic demand, but she did as he asked, taking a step back.

This is just a job and he's your employer, she repeated to herself like a mantra.

Those impenetrable grey eyes raked her up and down. He walked around her, and even though she'd endured years of people inspecting her like a brood mare, she felt restless under Zafir's intense gaze. Self-conscious. The top of the liner which sat between her leg and the prosthesis suddenly felt itchy, and she had to stop herself from reaching down to touch it.

Zafir came and stood in front of her again, that gaze boring into her, making her skin heat up.

'Stunning,' he pronounced. 'You're per—'

'Don't say that word!' Kat interrupted in a rush, immediately regretting it when Zafir's eyes narrowed on her.

Of course Zafir ignored her. '*Perfect?* Well, you are.'

Kat felt very aware of her leg, and the discomfort of getting used to the new prosthesis. She felt like a fraud, and longed to pull the necklace off. The weight of it was oppressive now, and a panicky sensation was rising.

She couldn't do this.

She turned around and bent her head forward, saying tightly, 'Can you take it off, please?'

There was no movement for a second, but then Zafir's hands were at the back of her neck. She caught the diamond in her hands when the clasp was undone and turned around, holding it out to Zafir.

He was too close. Kat held up the necklace, silently begging Zafir to take it and put some space between them. Finally he did, and stepped aside to put it back safely in the box.

Kat immediately walked over to a window, needing the illusion of air at least. She put her hand to her throat and felt for a moment as if she wouldn't be surprised to see that the necklace had left some kind of a mark.

Like the mark Zafir left on you? Inside where no one can see?

The panic rose. Kat turned around and looked at Zafir, who was shutting the box again but watching her. So far they'd exchanged only a handful of words, but the silent communication between them was almost deafening. It was too much.

'I'm sorry,' she blurted out. 'I don't think I can do this after all.'

Zafir put his hands in his pockets, unperturbed by her outburst. 'You're a professional model. This is probably one of the easiest jobs you've ever been asked to do— walk amongst a crowd for a few hours over a handful of evenings.'

It was so much more than that.

Zafir's easy dismissal made Kat see red. 'I'm not a model any more, Zafir. I haven't done this in—' She stopped short of saying exactly how long and amended it to, 'Months.'

'I'm sure it's just like riding a bike,' he drawled infuriatingly.

Kat had to force oxygen to her brain by taking a big deep breath. Zafir had no idea what he was really asking of her, and she had no intention of revealing all to the man who had so casually stepped on her heart.

Thank God, she thought now, *I never actually told him I loved him.*

'Anyway,' he said, prowling closer to where she stood in fight-or-flight mode, 'it's too late. You've signed the contract and, as per your request, a sizeable sum of up-front money has been already wired to your nominated account. No doubt to fill the black hole your debt created. Unless, of course,' he added silkily, 'you want to give the money back?'

Kat sagged. For a moment she'd forgotten. The money wasn't to fill a debt hole—it was going straight to the rehabilitation clinic, whom she'd already informed about their unexpected windfall, much to their delight and relief. And to Julie, to reimburse her for what she'd paid for the cosmetic limb. Kat had insisted, in spite of Julie's protests, wanting to feel as if she was at least starting to make her own way again.

So, yes, it *was* too late.

Straightening her shoulders, she called upon the inner strength she'd never known she possessed until recently and said, 'No, I'm not giving the money back and, yes, I've agreed to the job so I'll keep my word. I'm going to change into my own clothes now, and then I'd like to go home.'

Zafir frowned. 'I've booked this suite for you for tonight and tomorrow night—until we leave for Europe.'

Kat shook her head firmly. 'No. I'm going back to my apartment tonight. There are still some things I need to pack, and I've got one last shift at the restaurant this evening.'

Zafir's eyes flashed. 'You are *not* working in that restaurant another minute. And my driver can wait for you and bring you back here when you're ready.'

This was what Zafir had done before, and she'd been too awed to say no.

'You're moving in with me, I want you in my bed when I wake up in the morning, Kat.'

A summons she'd been only too happy to comply with.

'Please do not tell me what I can and can't do, Zafir. I'm not officially working for you until tomorrow, when I will be here at the appropriate time to start preparing for the first function.'

She tore her gaze away from his and walked with as much grace as she could muster to the bedroom, shutting the door firmly behind her and resting against it for a moment.

Her heart was pounding. Underneath all Zafir's arrogance she could feel his compelling pull, asking her for so much more. It had been explicit in the way he'd looked at her wearing the diamond. As if he wanted to devour her. No wonder she'd panicked for a moment.

Was that why he'd dismissed all his staff? Had he really believed that that's all it would take? Seeing him, being enticed with the rarest jewel in the world, she'd fall back into his bed—except this time without any illusion that he wanted more than a finite affair.

This time there would be no marriage proposal to kick the earth from under her legs, making her feel for the first time in her life as if she truly was worth something to someone... She'd believed that Zafir had really wanted her and loved her for herself, and not just for the aesthetically pleasing sum of her parts.

Kat struggled with the zip on the dress, but she was damned if she was going to emit so much as a squeak to let Zafir know she might need help. Eventually she managed to get it down, after some serious body contortions, and stripped off to get back into her own clothes.

She caught a glimpse of herself in a mirror and stopped for a moment, reminded of the fact that at first glance no one would see anything amiss but that on closer inspection they'd see her leg, and frown, and think, *Wait a second...*

Kat went cold all over as she contemplated Zafir ever seeing her like this—naked and exposed, her wounds visible.

Suddenly conscious that he was mere feet away, and separated from her only by a door, Kat stopped dithering and got dressed in her own clothes again, before going into the bathroom to wash off the make-up.

When her face was clean she straightened up and looked at herself. This was her now. Unadorned. She was naturally pale, and her hair tumbled around her shoulders, messy after she'd brushed it so roughly and darker in hue than she'd had it before, with natural copper highlights. She could see the faint lines wrought on her face already—the marks of her experience. Marks of her new strength, which she'd never needed more than now.

Zafir only wanted her when she appeared as she just had—when she was Kat the Supermodel.

As long as she could keep him at arm's length and show him that she wasn't the same woman, he'd soon lose interest and move on to someone far easier and more docile. As she'd once been. And when Zafir did lose interest and move on she'd finally be able to let go of the ties that still bound her to him like a spider's resilient silken threads, because his behaviour would confirm for her that all he'd ever been interested in was the illusion of the perfect woman.

A small voice whispered to Kat that all she had to do was take off her jeans, walk out of the bedroom and show

Zafir exactly who she was. He'd never want anything to do with her when he saw that she wasn't everything she'd once been. He could handle the potentially negative PR fallout, but he surely wouldn't want to seduce an ex-lover who was now an amputee.

So why don't you just do it, then? crowed that inner voice. *Go on—walk out of here and show him who you are now.*

Kat's hands gripped the sink hard. Her gut churned. If she did, it would all be over. She'd have to give the money back. She'd have to go to the rehab centre and apologise for getting their hopes up.

She took a deep breath, forcing herself to be calm. She was overreacting. Panicking. She didn't owe Zafir anything. She didn't owe him any explanations. He would lose interest once he realised that Kat would resist him no matter what. A man like Zafir didn't want a strong, opinionated woman. He wanted someone who wouldn't challenge him.

She could do this. She *would* do this. And when she walked away from Zafir after this was over, it would be for good.

Zafir handed over the diamond in its box to Noor and her security team. When he'd closed the door behind them he paced up and down restlessly.

Kat was seriously perplexing him. The fact that she'd choose going back to her rundown neighbourhood over sleeping in luxury was simply inexplicable. Not to mention wanting to fulfil one last shift at that excuse for a restaurant.

Once he'd known that she'd acquiesced to the job, he'd assumed that it meant that she was also agreeing to share his bed again. After all, he'd made it explicitly clear that he wanted her. And he knew she still wanted him—it throbbed in the air between them like live electricity.

He scowled at the closed bedroom door. So what was she up to? The sum of money she'd already received was enough for her to seriously upgrade her life. And yet just now, when he'd reminded her that it was too late for her to walk away, it had almost seemed as if she was reluctantly agreeing to commit to something burdensome— not embarking on a journey to one of the easiest paydays she'd ever had in her life.

He had to admit to a niggle of doubt that it was the money she was really interested in, even though he'd long ago come to the conclusion that Kat had refrained from telling him about her massive debt because she'd figured that once they were married he'd have no choice but to clear it for her.

He'd lavished her with gifts, yes, but she'd never seemed as enthralled by them as other women had. She'd get embarrassed, or try to convince him she didn't need whatever trinket he'd given her. When he'd given her underwear she'd blushed—and just thinking of that now made his body hard.

He went over to the window to look out broodingly. In the aftermath of their last bitter argument he'd summed their relationship up as nothing more than an elaborate act. Kat had been canny enough to try and secure a permanent position in his life before revealing the skeletons in her closet. In a way, with her coming from the background she had, he couldn't really blame her for developing such survival instincts...

He heard the bedroom door open and turned around to see her emerging, dressed down in a plaid shirt and faded jeans. Sneakers. Her hair was loose, the luxuriant waves tumbling around her shoulders, and his blood leapt. He realised that he preferred it like this—darker. It made her beauty somehow more dramatic, mature.

She was pulling a wheelie suitcase behind her and she caught his look and said defensively, 'I'm not staying. This is full of the accessories I told the stylists I'd bring from home.'

The uncomfortable assertion that she really wasn't playing hard to get made Zafir's skin prickle. He walked across the room and saw how she tensed visibly, her hand clutching the handle of the suitcase. It made something deep inside him roar like an animal. He knew this woman intimately. He'd been her first lover...the first man to bring her to orgasm...

A sense of extreme exposure that he wanted her so much—so much that he'd brought her back into his life and precipitated all these questions—propelled Zafir forward until he had both Kat's arms in his hands. He barely noticed the suitcase fall to the side because she was no longer holding it.

She was looking up at him, two spots of pink in her cheeks, her eyes huge and wary. Gold and green.

Something dark rose up inside him and he couldn't hold it back.

'How many have there been, Kat? How many men have you lain down for and fooled into believing that you're just a regular woman? Did they know who they were sleeping with? That the woman with her legs wrapped around their hips was really—'

'Stop it.'

Kat was as rigid as a board under his hands. 'How dare you? Who I have or haven't slept with is none of your business. I don't want the sordid details of your lovers, who I've no doubt you made sure met your exacting standards of moral integrity.'

Zafir's pulse thundered as Kat's sweetly evocative

scent tantalised him. The only woman he wanted was glaring at him and shooting gold sparks from her eyes.

He forced out through the hunger raging in his blood, 'Quite frankly, I'm a lot less fixated on moral integrity this time around.'

A shiver ran through Kat's body and Zafir felt it.

'There is no *this time*. This is just a job for me—that's all. I'm not interested in anything else.'

Everything in Zafir rejected that, and he lifted one hand to cup Kat's delicate jawline. Just the silken brush of her hair against the back of his hand had his body hardening all over again.

'Why are you denying this, Kat? Whatever is between us, it's mutual. And it's even stronger than before.'

She shook her head. 'It's not mutual.'

'Liar,' Zafir breathed, as every part of his body went on fire with an urgent and undeniable desire to prove Kat wrong. And along with that desire he felt something much more dangerous: *emotion*.

To block it out, deny it, Zafir cupped his hand behind Kat's neck and drew her to him until he could feel the length of her willowy body pressed against his.

Her hands came up between them to his chest. The wariness and anger was gone, to be replaced by something far more like panic. And why would she be panicky unless he was about to prove her very wrong?

'Zafir, what are you doing?'

His blood was pounding. 'I'm proving that once a liar, always a liar...'

And then he bent his head and covered Kat's mouth with his, and for the first time in eighteen months the roaring savage heat inside him was momentarily soothed.

Under the intense carnal satisfaction to be tasting her again was that emotion and a kind of relief. As if he'd found his way back to some place he'd been looking for.

It was so profound and overwhelming that for long seconds Zafir didn't even deepen the kiss—he just relished the sensation of Kat's soft, lush mouth under his.

And then she made a soft mewling sound and Zafir fell over the brink of his control and hauled Kat even closer, kissing her deep enough to see stars.

Time stood still. The earth might have stopped rotating. All Zafir was aware of was the feel of Kat's curves against his body, the stiffness of his arousal cushioned against her soft belly...and the desire to stop at nothing until he was deeply embedded between her legs and she was crying out his name as her climax sent them both into orbit.

It took a second for Zafir to realise that Kat had torn her mouth away and was pushing against his chest, breathing heavily enough for him to feel her breasts move against him. He almost growled. He felt feral.

She pushed hard and dislodged Zafir's arms, stumbling slightly as she stepped back. Her eyes were molten, her mouth was swollen and her cheeks were flushed, and the only thing keeping Zafir from reaching for her again was the knowledge that he'd already exposed himself.

'I do not want this, Zafir. I won't deny that the attraction between us is still there—'

Zafir snorted at the understatement and Kat's eyes turned steely.

'But I am not going there with you again. We had our moment and it's over. And unless you can promise to keep things between us on a professional footing I'll have no choice but to back out of our agreement and return the money you've already paid me. Don't think I won't, Zafir. The money is important to me, but not as important as not making the same mistake twice.'

No one spoke to Zafir like this. No one considered him a mistake.

But then an echo of his brother's voice whispered from the past, angry...

'Sara was a mistake, Zafir, our parents didn't even pretend to grieve when she died. Her life had no value because she couldn't rule when she came of age. They betrayed her more than you'll ever understand...'

Zafir pushed the past away, and with it the familiar ache of longing and disconnection. That ache shamed him, because he was above such weakness, or should be. He had to be. And he also ruthlessly shut out the niggling pain that his brother hadn't confided in him more.

Salim had shut Zafir out long ago, pursuing a life of debauched irresponsibility. Laughing in the face of his responsibilities. It was love that had done that to his brother—albeit sibling love. The twins had had their own little world, exclusive to everyone around them—even Zafir. And after Sara had died Salim had never been the same.

Seeing his brother's reaction to Sara's death, witnessing the pain of losing that intense bond, had bred within Zafir a lifelong desire to protect himself against such deep investment in another person. It appalled him that you could lose yourself like that.

Kat was looking at him now, and Zafir took a step back—as much from the intensity flowing between them as from his unwelcome reflections. He didn't appreciate Kat's ultimatum, but at the same time he didn't want to reveal the extent of his need. He'd already revealed too much. However, he could not let her rewrite their history.

He folded his arms. 'What happened between us was not a mistake, Kat. We were both adults, acting on mutual desire. The fact that it ended as it did was as much your responsibility as it was mine. You kept truths from me and I shouldn't have trusted you so easily.'

Kat seemed to go pale in the low lights of the room. 'Let's just leave it at that, then.'

Something in Zafir rebelled at that. 'By all means—if you think we can leave the past in the past. I, however, happen to believe that sooner or later you'll have to admit we have a present too.'

Kat bent down and picked up the handle of her suitcase. She looked at Zafir. 'The only present we have is a professional one, Zafir.'

For now, he told himself silently as he came forward and took Kat's suitcase out of her hand, leading her out of the suite and to his car downstairs.

She got into the car without looking at him once, keeping her face averted. Only that lingering sense of exposure stopped him from pulling her back out of the car to show her what a mockery this *professionalism* was.

He'd arrogantly assumed resuming a physical relationship with Kat would be easy. He couldn't have been more wrong. And yet he wasn't dissuaded. If anything, this pared down and feisty Kat was sparking his desire in a far deeper way than she ever had before.

As he watched his car slide away from the kerb and into the evening traffic he told himself that she wouldn't be able to hold out against this insane chemistry for long.

CHAPTER FOUR

'KAT, YOU LOOK...AMAZING.'

Kat heard the thickness in her friend's voice and tried not to let it affect her. She was having a hard enough time just breathing, and said shakily, 'Jules, I really don't know if I'm ready for this.'

Julie came and stood between Kat and the full-length mirror in the hotel suite bedroom, where Kat had returned some hours ago with her bags packed for the trip. They would leave tomorrow for London.

Kat was wearing the black velvet dress again. Her hair was in the chignon and her make-up had just been completed. Everyone had left, so now it was just the two of them.

Her petite blonde friend took Kat's hand in a firm grip and looked up at her steadily. 'I wouldn't push you if you weren't ready, Kat. But you are. You can't keep hiding from the world.'

Kat bit her lip to stop herself asking plaintively, *But this job? Now?* She looked at her reflection over her friend's head and saw the panicked look in her eyes, and forced herself to take in a breath.

Just then there was a knock on the door. Kat loved her friend for not jumping to answer it immediately, waiting to get a nod from Kat first. Gratitude made her chest swell because she knew that if she truly wanted to walk out of here right now her friend would support her. But she didn't want to let her down. And she didn't want to let the rehab centre down.

She could do this.

Before Julie had even opened the door Kat knew who it

was. Heat prickled over her skin. And, sure enough, when it swung back Zafir was there, filling the space effortlessly. He was dressed in a tuxedo and he was ridiculously gorgeous. And, even though Kat had seen him dressed like this before, it was still a shock to the system to behold such a formidable specimen of masculine perfection.

It was also the first time she'd seen him since yesterday, and the memory of that kiss made her pulse pound unevenly. Coming to terms with the resurrection of her sexual awareness was something she really hadn't expected to have to deal with for a long time. And yet it rushed through her now like an unstoppable wave.

Zafir was holding the necklace in his hand and he lifted it up. 'May I?'

Kat nodded dumbly and tensed against Zafir's effect on her as he walked in and came behind her, raising his hands up and over her head so that he could tie the clasp at the back of her neck.

The necklace felt warm and heavy against her skin and Kat touched it unconsciously. Julie's blue eyes had grown comically large and round as she took in the gem nestling against Kat's skin.

Kat looked at her reflection in the mirror and for a moment she was mesmerised too by the glowing red heart-shaped jewel. It did look somehow *alive*.

And then she raised her eyes and her gaze snagged on Zafir's. Those dark grey depths were focused solely on her. Not even looking at the gem. She swallowed. He was very close behind her, she could feel his heat, and only for the fact that Julie was still there, effectively acting as chaperone, stopped Kat from taking a step away.

He was the one finally to step back, and Kat breathed in shakily.

He went and stood beside Julie. 'You look stunning.'

She was glad he hadn't said *perfect*.

He extended his arm towards the door. 'Shall we? My driver is waiting.'

As Kat stepped forward her friend touched her arm and mouthed *good luck*. And then it was just Kat and Zafir, stepping out of the suite to where the security team were waiting, looking serious and alert.

Noor got into the elevator with them, and Kat was relieved not to be alone in the small space with Zafir. When they got out on ground level they were ushered straight to Zafir's car, and Kat instinctively arranged the long dress over her left leg, conscious of her prosthetic limb. It had been a long time since she'd felt so undressed.

Thankfully Zafir had to take a call on his mobile as they cut through the early-evening Manhattan traffic, giving Kat time to gather herself before entering back into the fray in spectacular fashion.

By the time they pulled up in front of the iconic Metropolitan Museum Zafir was off his phone, and the palms of her hands were clammy with sweat. It got worse when she saw the hordes of paparazzi and reporters and other people already lining the red carpet in their finery.

Zafir touched her bare arm and she looked at him.

'Okay?'

Kat nodded jerkily. 'Fine.'

She'd never been less fine in her life.

'Just follow my lead.'

Zafir got out of the car then, and came around to Kat's side, opening the door and helping her out. Once again she was glad of the dress disguising her leg as she stood up and wobbled for a moment. Zafir's hand was on her arm again, holding her steady.

She stepped up onto the sidewalk and they moved forward. As people noticed who they were a hush seemed to fall over the crowd for a split-second, and then all hell broke loose as they walked onto the red carpet.

Zafir had tucked Kat's arm over his and she wasn't aware of how tightly she was holding on, she was being blinded by all the bright flashes going off in her face.

For a moment she was paralysed, and then Zafir's deep voice sounded in her ear, saying calmly, 'Start walking and smile—that's all you have to do.'

And suddenly she was moving, propelled forward by Zafir. They stopped periodically to let photographers take pictures, and Zafir stood back to let Kat be photographed on her own.

After a few long torturous minutes Kat found herself relaxing slightly, as if a long unused muscle was coming back to life. She knew how to do this—how to project a smiling façade. She'd done it for years. And slowly the ability returned.

And then someone shouted out, 'Where have you been, Kat? Are you and Zafir back together?' and all her fragile confidence shattered.

She stumbled, but Zafir was there in an instant, steadying her again. He replied to the questions smoothly and authoritatively.

'Persuading Kat Winters out of retirement was an unexpected coup and we're delighted she's working with us for this diplomatic trip. As for our relationship—that's none of anyone's business except our own.'

Eventually they reached the end of the red carpet. Kat was ready to crawl under a rock, but the evening hadn't even started yet. And she was angry.

She pulled away from Zafir and looked up at him, saying in a low voice, 'You could have shut down their questions about our relationship more comprehensively.'

Zafir just looked at her explicitly. 'I could have.'

But I didn't.

He didn't have to bother saying that part. Before she could react, though, he put her arm firmly in his again and propelled her forward to the main entrance of the function room. Her anger dissolved into panic at the sight of the packed room.

He stopped there for a second and looked at her again. 'Ready?'

No! she wanted to blurt out, but if she turned and ran she'd only have to face the red carpet again. There was literally nowhere to go except forward.

Not liking how symbolic this moment felt, Kat nodded jerkily and they stepped over the threshold of the room, its doors being held open by pristinely uniformed butlers.

Much like the hush outside when they'd arrived, as soon as they stepped in through the doorway everyone turned to look and there was an audible intake of breath. Kat realised that a spotlight rested on her—undoubtedly it was to showcase the diamond, not her, but she still felt utterly exposed.

Zafir took her arm from his and stepped to the side, leaving her feeling ridiculously bereft for a second. Then she heard his strong voice say, 'May I present to you Kat Winters and the Heart of Jandor?'

The enthusiastic clapping and gasps of wonder at the sight of Kat and the gem had faded away, to be replaced by the excited chatter of hundreds of VIP guests.

Zafir noted the presence of high-ranking politicians mixed with award-winning actors and actresses, world champion athletes, prize-winning authors and everyone who was anyone with satisfaction. And yet his feeling of satisfaction somehow fell short.

He found he was more interested in where Kat was and with whom. Currently she was standing a few feet away from him, surrounded by a small goggle-eyed crowd. Irritated by this dent in his sense of satisfaction, Zafir cursed himself.

This was exactly what he'd envisaged, wasn't it? To have one of the most beautiful women in the world standing amongst an awed crowd as she showcased his country's famed jewel?

But if anything she outshone the diamond. The inky black of the dress and its clean lines showcased the perfection of Kat's body. No other jewellery. Understated make-up. And not a bump or a mark or a blemish to mar that lustrous skin.

Zafir didn't recall her being so pale before, but presumably if she hadn't been travelling to exotic locations for fashion shoots, as she'd used to, then she'd lost her natural golden tan. And yet her skin seemed to glow even more. Like a pearl.

She was in profile to him now, and his gaze scanned down from the abundant dark hair artfully arranged in its chignon, to her high forehead, straight nose, lush mouth, delicate jaw and long, graceful neck.

The rare gem sat just below her collarbone, glowing as if lit from within by fire. Her shoulders were slim and straight. And then, as if compelled by the beat of his blood, his hungry gaze dropped to the voluptuous swells of her breasts.

Blood rushed to his groin and Zafir had to grit his jaw and use all of his control to stop making a complete fool of himself. He snapped his gaze back to her face, which he could see now was tense. Smiling, but tense.

He recalled how tightly she'd gripped his arm while on the red carpet, and how she'd wobbled precariously a couple of times as if her legs were unsteady. And the strangest thing... When he'd announced her arrival a short while before and watched her stand tall but alone, bathed in the spotlight, he'd felt a curious sense of pride, without even knowing why, exactly.

She turned her head then, as if sensing his intense regard, and looked at him, and before Zafir was even aware of what he was doing he ignored the veritable queue of people Rahul had lined up to speak to him and walked to Kat's side.

Hours later Kat ached all over, and she sank down into the hot bath as much as she could, wishing she could submerge herself completely and forget how exposed she'd felt as she'd been paraded through that enormous room like a thoroughbred horse at a bloodstock auction.

And yet, to her surprise, Zafir had stayed by her side more or less constantly—even though she'd seen the frustration on his aide Rahul's face as he'd tried to entreat Zafir to talk to this person or that person.

She didn't like to admit that his presence had steadied her as much as it had unnerved her, and made her feel more capable of bearing up to the scrutiny—which had been of *her* as much as the gem. And that had been Zafir's cynical plan all along, hadn't it? To get the most out of bringing the notorious Kat Winters out of the woodwork?

Yet, a small voice pointed out, he hadn't had to stay by her side like that. He could have quite easily ignored her all night...

But before she went down the dangerous path of believing that he'd stayed by her side out of concern or anything more, she reminded herself that Zafir's motivations had undoubtedly been to make sure that she didn't damage the Jandor 'brand' or upstage the diamond. And also because he was still messing with her head, not letting her forget the sensual threat he'd made.

At the end of the evening Zafir had been pulled aside to talk to an emissary from the American foreign office, and Rahul had come to let Kat know that she could hand back the gem if she so wished. Like a coward, she'd seized the opportunity, and he'd accompanied her to an anteroom where Noor had overseen the return of the gem to its box and it had been whisked safely away.

Then, when they'd re-emerged into the function room and Kat had seen that Zafir was still in conversation, she'd told Rahul that she was ready to leave.

Immediately he'd looked worried and said nervously, 'I should check with the King—'

Kat had cut in more firmly than she'd felt, 'I'm quite tired, and we have an early start to get to London in time for the function tomorrow evening, I'm sure you wouldn't want the King to be displeased because I don't appear rested.'

She'd almost felt sorry for how conflicted Rahul had looked, but eventually he'd agreed and had accompanied her down to the car and seen her off.

She'd just been breathing a sigh of relief when she'd received a text from Zafir while still in the car.

Next time, we leave together, Kat. Get some rest for tomorrow. Rahul will escort you to the royal plane in the morning and I'll meet you there.

Kat hadn't appreciated being made to feel like an admonished child, and yet now her mind drifted back to how Zafir had looked amongst the crowd earlier, how effortlessly he'd stood out with his height and dark good looks.

She couldn't stop a pulse fluttering between her legs as she recalled how she'd caught him looking at her with something raw in his eyes. Raw, and hungry. It had leapt across the space from him to her, and she'd felt it as strongly as if he'd physically reached out and touched her.

The pulse between Kat's legs intensified and she shifted in the bath, putting her hand down there, almost as if she could try to stop it. But once her fingers came into contact with her sensitised skin and she felt how slippery she was she sucked in a pained breath.

She'd been on a knife-edge of desire all evening, as much as she'd tried to ignore it. But she couldn't any more, and her fingers moved tentatively but far too easily against herself, helped by the water and her own slick arousal.

She'd never touched herself like this…not until Zafir had shown her how and had instructed her to do it for him. She thought of that now—how he'd sat naked in a chair and told her to get on the bed and spread her legs, to show herself to him, and then to touch herself. He'd held himself in his hand as she'd done his bidding, his fist moving up and down the stiff column of flesh in a slow, relentless rhythm.

It had been the singularly most indecent and erotic thing she'd ever experienced, and just as she'd exploded into pieces around her own fingers Zafir had surged up, taken her hand away, seated himself between her legs and thrust into her, deep and hard, and had kept her falling over the edge again and again until she'd screamed herself hoarse.

Kat could feel herself quickening now, tightening, as her movements became more feverish and desperate… and yet in the same moment she realised that Zafir wasn't watching her this time. She was alone in a bath…dreaming of the past and a scenario that would never be repeated.

Disgusted with herself, she took her hand away and opened her eyes, breathing harshly, ignoring the ache between her legs and the way her nipples were so tight they hurt. The truth was that she knew she would find no real satisfaction like this, and it killed her to admit it.

Kat pushed herself upright from the water and balanced on one leg. She sat on the edge of the bath, swinging herself over before drying herself roughly and reaching for the crutches she had nearby. Then she manoeuvred herself to standing, excess water dripping onto the towels she'd placed on the floor to stop herself from slipping and sliding when she got out.

Getting out of a bath was a process that was second nature now, but it had taken many months to perfect. It never ceased to amaze and humble her how much she'd taken for granted before.

She deliberately avoided her reflection in the countless bathroom mirrors, feeling like a coward. But right now she didn't need a reminder of exactly why Zafir would never look at her with that same hungry raw need again.

And the sooner she shut down these inappropriate fantasies, the better. Or she wouldn't survive another day, never mind another couple of weeks.

The following day Zafir was still stewing over the fact that Kat had left the function without him last night.

They'd departed from New York early in the morning, nearly six hours ago, so their landing in London was imminent.

Rahul had brought her to the plane and Kat had looked pale and tight-lipped, answering any questions Zafir had posed with monosyllabic answers. And then, when he'd suggested that she take advantage of the bedroom to rest, she'd disappeared for the rest of the flight.

Zafir sighed moodily and took in the sea of endless clouds outside his window. He really wasn't used to being thwarted like this. Especially not when the sexual tension between them was off the charts. He'd seen the way her gaze had roved over him hungrily when she'd first stepped into the plane, as if she wasn't even aware of her impulse. Which was the same as his. To devour her with his eyes at every opportunity.

He heard a noise from the back and that ever-present desire spiked as Kat's evocative scent reached him just before she did. She sat down in her seat again, asking huskily, 'We're nearly there?'

Zafir did his best to clamp down on the need to reach over and pluck her bodily from her seat and into his lap. 'Yes,' he gritted out. 'Within the next half hour. We've started our descent.'

Rahul's staff were at the front of the plane—out of sight and earshot—and his greedy gaze took in Kat's soft jeans and the loose, unstructured top that somehow still managed to mould itself to her curves. Her hair was down, and Zafir wanted to wrap it around his hand and force her to look at him.

'You won't turn to stone if you look at me, Kat.'

He couldn't disguise the irritation lacing his words. He saw how she tensed, but then eventually she turned her head and those glorious golden, amber and green eyes settled on him. Cool. Unreadable. *Why* was she so reluctant to take what he was offering? A no-strings-attached, very adult exorcism of this palpable connection between them.

He turned in his seat more fully, to face her. 'You must be hungry. You haven't eaten because you were sleeping.'

Before she could say anything he'd called for a steward, who materialised immediately. Zafir looked at Kat expressively. For a moment a mutinous expression crossed her face, but then she seemed to give in and said to the staff member, 'I'll just have something light…like an omelette, if you have it?'

Zafir added an order for coffee for both of them and the steward left.

Looking disgruntled, Kat said, 'You're still too bossy. And arrogant.'

Zafir shrugged, unperturbed. 'I'm a King now. I have a licence to be as bossy and arrogant as I want.'

Suddenly Kat looked stricken, and those eyes which had been so unreadable were now full of something far more readable. Sympathy.

'I never mentioned your father. I'm sorry for your loss. I know you weren't particularly close, but still it can't have been easy.'

Zafir's insides clenched. Plenty of people had offered empty platitudes when his father had died, but few had known just how barren their relationship had been. But he'd told Kat. And her simple sincerity now tugged on a deep part of him that *had* mourned his father—or at least mourned the fact that he'd never been a father in the real sense. The loving sense.

The steward arrived then, with Kat's food and the coffees, and Zafir said gruffly, 'Eat. We'll be landing soon and we have a busy schedule this evening.'

After a few moments Kat picked up her cutlery and ate with single-minded absorption.

When she'd finished, he mused out loud, 'You always did have a good appetite.'

Kat went still and pushed the plate away from her before taking up her cup of coffee. She glanced at Zafir without letting him see her eyes properly. Her mouth had gone tight and she said, 'When you grow up hungry it gives you an appreciation of food that others might not have.'

'Was it really that bad, Kat?'

She glared at him. 'You read that article along with everyone else in America, didn't you? The lurid details of my life in a trailer park?'

Zafir shook his head, his irritation mounting. 'I still don't know why you couldn't tell me the full details. There's no shame in growing up poor, *or* in a trailer park.'

'No,' she said, avoiding his eyes again. 'Only in the choices we make to survive.'

Kat felt bitterness corrode her insides even as she knew that this was her chance to spill it all out to Zafir. He was listening and receptive, and she'd always wanted to tell him, hadn't she? But suddenly the thought of laying it all out felt too huge. She still felt vulnerable after appearing in public again for the first time last night, and like a coward she clammed up, avoiding the opportunity.

Instead she looked at him and said, 'You called me a liar the other day, but I never lied to you. I just…didn't tell you everything.'

'A distinction that hardly exonerates you,' Zafir pointed out.

He felt frustration mount when she didn't respond, aware of a niggling sensation that she was still hiding things from him.

Just then the air steward arrived to clear Kat's plate and inform them that they'd be landing shortly, and to make sure they were ready. The tension dissipated and Kat broke their staring contest to turn her head and look out of her window.

The plane circled lower and lower over the private London airfield and Zafir addressed his question to the back of Kat's glossy head, unable to resist pushing her for a response. 'You never told me why you didn't go back into modelling full-time once you'd recovered.'

Zafir could feel her reluctance as she finally turned to look at him again, eyes guarded.

'It wasn't a career I'd ever really chosen for myself, and I discovered that if I had the choice I wouldn't necessarily step back into it.'

Which was more or less the truth, Kat reassured herself as Zafir's incisive gaze seemed to laser all the way into her soul. Even if she hadn't lost her leg she wouldn't have wanted to step back into that vacuous world. Being forced out of her old existence and into a new one had revealed a desire to find a more meaningful role in her life. What that might be, she wasn't even sure herself yet. She only knew that she wanted to help people as she had been helped...

The plane touched down with a brief jolt and Zafir finally looked away. Released from that compelling gaze, Kat took a breath. She'd tried to rest earlier, in the plane's luxurious bedroom, but sleep had proved elusive. She was too wound up after those illicit fantasies in her bath last night and the prospect of another public exhibition this evening.

Perhaps, she thought to herself a little hysterically, this was Zafir's retribution? Expose Kat to the ravenous judgmental hordes who would pick her over until there was nothing left?

Although, from what she'd seen of the headlines in the papers that Rahul had been poring over in the car earlier, there didn't seem to be much dredging up of the past—only feverish speculation as to why Kat had re-emerged and where she'd been and the nature of her relationship with Zafir. Kat wasn't sure whether to be relieved or even more anxious at the thought that someone from the rehabilitation clinic might recognise her and sell the story of what had really happened to her.

Before she could dwell on that too much Zafir was standing, holding her bag in one hand and his other hand out to her. She looked at it for a moment, and then realised how futile it would be to try and resist. She put her hand in Zafir's and let him pull her up. She stumbled slightly, falling against Zafir's chest. His eyes flared and his hand came up to steady her, curling around her arm tightly.

For a moment their bodies were welded together and the heat between them surged.

Roughly he said, 'Kat, why can't you just admit—'

'Sire, the cars are ready.'

Zafir clamped his mouth shut and didn't look around at Rahul, their interrupter.

Relief flooded Kat, because she realised that if Zafir had kissed her in that moment she'd have responded helplessly. She pulled free and walked to the entrance of the plane, taking care on the steps down, telling herself it was her prosthetic limb and not the throbbing arousal rushing through her body making her feel wobbly.

The event in London was even more impressive than the one in New York. Because of Zafir's royal status, senior members of the British royal family were present, imbuing the classic surroundings of one of London's oldest and most exclusive hotels with an elegance and gravitas Kat had never experienced before.

The ornate furnishings glittered under the flickering glow of hundreds of candles. A string quartet played on a dais at one end of the room. Pristine waiters moved silently and discreetly through the crowd, offering tantalising, exotic hors d'oeuvres prepared by Zafir's Jandori chef and glasses of priceless champagne.

Tonight Kat was dressed in a long strapless white dress. A sheath of simplicity which helped to show the red diamond to its best advantage. Zafir hadn't arrived at her suite to put the diamond around her neck earlier—it had been a stylist who had taken it from one of Noor's guards to place around her neck—and Kat denied furiously to herself that she'd missed his presence and his touch.

When Rahul had met her to walk her down to the function room, which was in the same hotel where they would stay the night, he'd explained that Zafir had had to take an important conference call and sent his apologies.

She'd denied the little dart of disappointment and

she'd ruthlessly quashed the relief she'd felt to see Zafir waiting outside the function room—pacing, actually—dressed once again in a classic tuxedo that did nothing to disguise his virile masculinity and everything to enhance it.

His gaze had swept her up and down. This evening her hair was tamed into a sleek bun, low at the back of her head, and she'd seen Zafir's gaze rest on it and how his eyes had flared with something unreadable. In that moment she'd gone breathless, imagining that she could almost feel his desire to undo it and let her hair fall down in its habitual unruly tumble of waves. He'd always loved it down...and the memory of that had made her weak.

But then he'd extended his arm, and she'd walked forward as the doors had opened and they'd stepped through.

And now Kat was standing beside Zafir on a small podium as he spoke to the hushed crowd and told them of the myriad opportunities available for business and recreation in his country. Kat found herself forgetting that she was under a spotlight while Zafir's deep and hypnotic voice painted a seductive picture of a land steeped in history and with boundless opportunities.

His love for his people and his country was evident in the passion in his voice, and she couldn't stop a dart of surprise and pride because she'd had no idea that Zafir was so determined to be a force for change in his country. The vision he outlined was modern and progressive, and was now being met with resounding applause.

She'd underestimated him, and that unsettled her as he stepped off the podium and held out a hand to help her down. She wasn't thinking, and she landed on her left leg a little awkwardly, wincing as the movement jarred her prosthesis. Any kind of steps, up or down, were more of a challenge than before.

Immediately he was sharp. 'Are you okay?'

'Fine—I just turned my ankle for a moment,' she embellished quickly.

Zafir frowned. 'Maybe we should have someone check it.'

Instant panic flooded her veins, turning her blood cold. 'No, I'm fine. Really.'

She spent the rest of the evening with a bright smile plastered on her face, even as her discomfort increased. She needed to take her prosthesis off to adjust it, but Zafir wouldn't leave her side and she was loath to attract his attention.

Finally, when she was wondering if the evening would ever end, the crowd thinned out and Zafir said, 'I'll take you to your suite and you can give the necklace back to the security guards for the night.'

Relief made her almost dizzy as he accompanied her out of the room and up in the elevator, with the ever-present Noor. Kat could be thankful for at least that much. As long as she wore the diamond, she wouldn't be alone with Zafir.

Once in Kat's suite, Noor stood at a respectful distance as Zafir took off the necklace and placed it into the box before handing it over.

Noor bowed her head. 'Good night, Sire... Miss Winters.'

She left the room and they were alone. Before Kat could say a word, though, Zafir put his hands on her shoulders and turned her around so she had her back to him. Then his hands were on her hair, plucking out the pins that had been holding the tight bun in place. As she felt it loosen and start to unravel, the discomfort of her limb was forgotten momentarily at the sheer bliss of *this*... Zafir's hands moving through her hair, massaging her skull.

His voice was low, husky. 'I've imagined doing this all evening.'

His body was close behind her and she could feel his heat and the whipcord strength of him. So close. So seductive. Treacherously, something gave way inside her, as if it was too strong for her to keep holding it back. Almost without realising what she was doing, she turned and looked up.

Zafir went still. Kat was looking up at him, eyes wide and molten, cheeks flushed. Every instinct within him called for him to claim her—finally. But something stopped him…a memory, brutally vivid and brutally exposing.

Kat sensed the chill even before she saw the heat in Zafir's eyes disappear. He dropped his hands and stepped back. She blinked, feeling vulnerable and hating herself for that small moment when he must have seen her desire laid bare.

When Zafir spoke he sounded harsh. 'Go to bed, Kat. I have some meetings here in the morning. Rahul will accompany you to the airport after lunch.'

And then he turned and walked out, the door closing behind him with an incongruously soft click.

Kat felt a little dazed, not sure what had just happened. She looked around and sank down onto the nearest chair. She could feel the discomfort in her leg again, and pulled up her dress in order to start taking off her prosthetic limb. But then she stopped, realising she needed to get her crutches first.

Feeling seriously on edge and irritable, she went into the bedroom, cursing Zafir for scrambling her brain so much that she forgot the fundamental basics.

But what irritated her the most, as she retrieved her crutches and started to undress so she could take off her prosthesis, was the fact that if he hadn't pulled back just now she'd most likely be on the nearest horizontal surface, giving up all her secrets to Zafir in the most humiliating way possible.

And that wasn't even the worst thing—because the worst thing was the insidious need to know, why had he stopped?

CHAPTER FIVE

LONDON UNDER MOONLIGHT twinkled benignly outside Zafir's suite window, with all of the famous landmarks lit up: the London Eye, the Shard, the dome and spires of St Paul's cathedral. But he couldn't care less about any of them. Or the fact that so far his diplomatic tour was a resounding success.

His head was filled with only one thing. Recrimination for letting a mere memory stop him from seeking the relief his body ached for. That was the past—this was the present. And yet the two were colliding far too vividly for his liking.

But when Kat had looked at him just now the sense of déjà vu had been strong enough to propel him out of her orbit. Déjà vu of the moment he'd proposed to her...

As much as Zafir would have liked to believe his proposal had been a well thought out and strategic move, it hadn't been. It had been spontaneous—not a behaviour that usually dictated his actions. They'd been travelling in his private jet, from London back to New York, and as he'd watched Kat across the aisle, staring dreamily out of the window, with his blood still humming after an overload of recent carnal satisfaction, she'd turned her head to look at him and he'd been overcome with a desperate and inexplicable need to ensure she never left his sight. And so he'd proposed, surprising her as much as himself.

He cursed himself now and turned from the view not liking the reminder that his proposal had been far less strategic than he liked to admit. He strode into the bedroom, shedding clothes as he went until he was naked.

When he reached the bathroom he stepped into the shower and turned it on. To cold.

He cursed volubly as the freezing water hit his skin, but it did little to douse the fever in his blood or the unwelcome memories in his head. He should have just followed his instincts and taken her. She wouldn't have stopped him this time—he felt it deep in his gut. And lower, where he still ached in spite of the cold water.

If anything, Kat had only proved that her defiance and reluctance were an act, and that she was biding her time before giving in. It was a little power play...she was messing with his head.

Next time he wouldn't let anything stop him, and when this tour was over and he'd slaked his lust he *would* walk away from Kat, and he would not feel the slightest ounce of regret because she'd be relegated to the past for good.

'Dinner, Kat. It's a social construct designed for people to sit down together and make conversation. Break bread together.'

Kat looked at Zafir suspiciously where he stood on the other side of her Parisian hotel suite's door. The Paris event wasn't due to take place until the following evening, and Kat had been savouring the thought of some breathing space while Zafir had meetings at the Jandor consulate nearby. She'd been looking forward to an early evening in bed, with a view of the Eiffel tower outside her window, watching old movies and eating ice-cream— her comfort staples. But now her peace was shattered.

'I know what dinner is.' She tried to keep her tone even. 'But what do you want to talk about? We have nothing to discuss.'

Zafir leaned a shoulder against the doorframe, supremely relaxed. Supremely dangerous. 'We're friends at least—aren't we, Kat?'

She scowled. 'You're my employer and I'm your employee.'

'We have history,' he countered.

'*Ancient* history,' she blasted back, panic rising as she realised that the past felt far too close for comfort. This Zafir was the one she remembered and feared. Relentless, seductive. Impossible to resist.

'We're ex-lovers,' he said silkily. 'I'd say we have plenty to talk about.'

And just like that a slideshow of explicit images bombarded Kat's memory banks, rendering her speechless.

As if sensing her momentary weakness, Zafir straightened from the door and said, 'I'll come back for you in an hour, Kat. Be ready.'

He was leaving before she could wrap her tongue around another word, but then he stopped abruptly and came back. 'Actually, I was going to go for a run, if you'd like to join me?'

A sharp pain lanced Kat right in the gut. She and Zafir used to jog together all the time. She'd taken great delight in keeping up with his punishing regular five-mile regime.

She felt hollow inside as she shook her head firmly. 'No, thank you.'

Zafir shrugged minutely and backed away again, oblivious to the turmoil caused by his easy invitation. 'As you wish—see you in an hour.'

She finally shut the door on his retreating back, and leant against it, an awful poignancy making her chest swell with emotion. Before it could turn into anything more she issued an unladylike curse and pushed herself away from the door.

The prospect of an evening with Zafir loomed large. The hollow feeling dissipated, to be replaced with a predictable array of physical reactions at the thought of sitting down with him one on one. Her skin grew hot, her pulse tripled and butterflies swarmed into her belly against her best efforts to quell his effect on her.

He was chipping away at the walls she'd erected around herself and he wasn't even aware of it. Yesterday evening she'd come so close to succumbing, and only because of *his* self-control she'd been saved from outright humiliation.

Damn him and his games. Damn him and his easy invitation to do something she'd never easily do again.

But he doesn't know about your leg, reminded a chiding voice.

And he never would, she vowed now. Because if he did it would mean he'd breached her last defences.

She walked over to the closet and opened the doors, purposely picking out the most casual clothes she possessed.

But when Zafir appeared at her door again, in exactly an hour's time, he looked smart and gorgeous in a dark suit, with his shirt open at the neck, and she felt like a rebellious teenager. His explicit look told her what he thought of the soft leather trousers, flat ankle boots and the loose, unstructured grey top. She'd left her hair down, wore minimal make-up, and reached for her light wraparound jacket and bag before coming into the hall and closing the door behind her.

Zafir appeared amused, which made her feel even more exposed and silly. 'Don't worry, Kat. I won't get the wrong idea, if that's what you're afraid of.'

He stood back to let her precede him into the elevator, and as it descended he leant against one mirrored wall with his hands in his pockets.

'You used to love wearing short skirts and high heels,' he observed. 'Is this some new feminist stance or is it just to ward me off?'

Kat's insides turned to ice. She *had* loved wearing the highest of heels and the shortest of dresses and skirts. And only ever for this man, because the carnal hunger and appreciation in his gaze had used to make her feel sexy and desired.

Relief warred confusingly with disappointment to hear that Zafir would obviously prefer to see her dressing as she'd used to.

Feeling exposed, she rounded on him, saying heatedly, 'No, it's not a feminist stance, actually. Women *should* be able to wear whatever they want—and not to entice a man. For themselves.'

He wasn't perturbed by her outburst. As the elevator doors opened he said easily, 'I was merely making an observation, not stating a preference, and I agree with you one hundred per cent. For what it's worth, Kat, you could wear a sack from head to toe and it wouldn't diminish how much I want you.'

Before she could respond to that, he took her arm in a loose but proprietorial hold to guide her across the exclusive Paris hotel lobby and out through the doors to his chauffeur-driven car.

She barely noticed the ubiquitous security vehicle waiting to tail their every move. Zafir had blindsided her a little. She'd always pegged him as being unremittingly traditional and conservative because he was so effortlessly alpha, but maybe that wasn't fair.

When they were settled in the back of his car she asked, 'Where are we going?'

He looked at her, his face cast into shadow, making it stern and even more compelling. 'It's a surprise.'

Kat's insides clenched. She had a feeling she knew exactly where, and if she was right she wanted to jump out of the car right now. Zafir had introduced her to a restaurant here on their first trip to Paris, shortly after they'd started seeing each other, and the experience was seared into her memory.

It was one of the city's oldest establishments, famous for its decadent furnishings and for its private dining rooms, which had been used in previous centuries for clandestine assignations of a very carnal nature. Zafir had, of course, booked one of those rooms, and Kat's memories of the evening had nothing to do with the food they'd eaten and everything to do with the wicked pleasures he'd subjected her to in the intimate and luxuriously furnished space...

She refused to let Zafir guess how agitated she was by these memories and looked out of the window, taking in the glittering lights and beautiful buildings. She'd always loved Paris as it had been the first place she'd visited outside of America in her early modelling days. Its beauty and history had astounded her, and nowhere else had ever had the same effect on her.

Her conscience twinged... Except for Jahor, the awe-inspiring capital city of Zafir's country, Jandor. It sprawled across a series of hills, overlooking the sparkling sea, and the skyline was made up of minarets and flat roofs, with children flying multicoloured kites as the sun went down. Overlooking it all was the golden-hued grand palace.

'We're here.'

Kat came out of the past and frantically checked where they were, a sigh of relief moving through her when she realised they weren't at the restaurant she'd been thinking of. Instead, as Zafir came around and helped her out of the car, she saw that they were in a small street on Île de la Cité—one of Paris's many small islands in the Seine.

Intrigued in spite of herself, she let Zafir lead her over to a small restaurant tucked between two tall buildings. From the outside it looked inviting, with golden light spilling out onto the street. And it was not like anywhere Zafir had ever brought her before.

In fact when he spoke he sounded almost…uncertain. 'This is one of Paris's best kept secrets.'

Kat looked at him and said drily, 'Were you expecting me to throw a tantrum because it's not a restaurant three hundred storeys up with a view of the Eiffel Tower?'

Zafir was unreadable, 'I'm not sure what to expect any more.'

Before she could respond, he was leading her into the restaurant. She was surprised to see that he got a warm welcome from the proprietor, who greeted Zafir like a long-lost son and her like an old friend.

Within seconds their coats had been taken and they were seated in a discreet corner, tucked away but able to see everything. The table was small, but exquisitely set with a white tablecloth and silver cutlery. Soft music played in the background and every other table was full, everyone engrossed in each other. It was achingly and effortlessly romantic.

Feeling vulnerable and defensive, Kat said, 'I wouldn't have thought this was your kind of place.'

Zafir shook out his napkin and laid it across his lap before reaching for a bread roll. 'I worked here in the kitchen as an apprentice chef while I was at the Sorbonne for a semester.'

Kat's jaw dropped. Zafir looked at her and smiled.

'Good to know I'm still capable of surprising you.'

Feeling even more vulnerable now, Kat said testily, 'You accused me of lying, but you weren't exactly forthcoming with information yourself.'

Zafir's smile faded and air between them crackled. 'It wasn't talking about myself I was most interested in where you were concerned.'

A waiter appeared then, and took their order, and he

was quickly followed by a sommelier who took their wine order. When the wine had been poured and they were alone again, Kat felt ridiculously self-conscious and aware of Zafir, his long legs bracketing hers beneath the table.

He sat back, the delicate stem of his wine glass between long fingers. 'Why did you do it, Kat?'

She looked at him, feeling panicked. 'What?'

His face was stark. 'The pictures. Why did you let a man see you like that when you were so young? Why weren't you in school?'

Kat's hand tightened on her glass. She hated that she still didn't feel ready to tell Zafir everything. She wondered if she ever would. '*Now* you want to know? It won't change anything.'

Their starter arrived—deliciously creamy mushroom soup with truffle oil. To Kat's relief, Zafir seemed happy to let the question go while they ate, and he told her some stories of working there under a famously mercurial chef.

She said, 'I had no idea you were interested in cooking. And why take a job when you didn't have to?'

'I may be privileged—'

Kat snorted indelicately at that understatement.

Zafir continued. 'But I soon got bored when I wasn't studying. I was walking past this place one day and saw a sign in the window advertising for kitchen help, so I applied. No one here knew who I was. To them I was just Zafir Noury, a foreign student. It was only when my bodyguards made themselves a little too noticeable that questions were asked. But they let me stay working here and protected my identity. When Marcel, the owner, got into financial difficulty some years ago I was able to help him out, so now I have a stake in the business too.'

Kat's jaw would have dropped again, but she kept her mouth firmly shut. This was a side to Zafir she'd never known existed. Happy to be anonymous. Not afraid of menial work. When she'd known him he'd been feted as the Crown Prince of Jandor, King in Waiting. Influential and imposing. Overwhelming.

To her surprise they fell into an easy conversation for the rest of the impeccably prepared meal. So when their plates had been cleared, and Kat was feeling semirelaxed in Zafir's company for the first time since she'd seen him again, and he repeated his question about those photos she felt almost betrayed. As if he'd been lulling her into a false sense of security on purpose.

Feeling prickly, because she knew she was being a coward, she said, 'What purpose will this serve, Zafir? You weren't interested in knowing before. Why now?'

He shrugged minutely. 'Let's just say that when you ran out of my apartment that night you left more questions than answers.'

Kat bit back the accusation that he'd not been remotely interested in hearing any explanations that night, because truly, how hard had she tried to get him to listen to her? Not hard at all. Not once she'd known how he really felt. Or *didn't* feel.

But she realised now that the time had come—ready or not—to tell him what she would have told him that night if she hadn't felt so betrayed by his admission that he didn't love her.

She took a breath and forced herself to look at him. 'By the time I was seventeen I was the main breadwinner. Thanks to the endless round of beauty pageants I'd been entered into ever since my mother realised my looks had currency, I was working almost full-time as a model and supporting us both. I badly needed money for her medical bills.'

Zafir frowned. 'Her drug use.'

Kat refused to let him intimidate her again. She said in a low, fierce voice, '*No*. I never funded her drug use. But no matter what I did, or how many rehab programmes I tried to get her onto, she always relapsed.' Kat could feel her cheeks grow hot with shame as she said, 'She used to steal from me to buy her drugs. No matter how careful I was, she always found the money.'

'But surely you had a bank account?'

'Yes,' Kat said tightly, 'but I was a minor, so she was the joint account holder. That was no safer place to hide my money than underneath my bed.'

Zafir's eyes flashed. 'You were a minor when that man took those photos.'

Kat felt bile rise when she thought of that awful day. A day when she'd crossed a line and knew she'd never feel clean again.

'My mother was in a bad way. She'd taken all my money and she'd almost overdosed to death. She was in hospital. My last resort was to try and get her into a private rehab facility...but it was expensive. This man—the photographer—he wasn't anyone I'd met before, but one of the girls I modelled with told me about him and about the money I could make...'

'If you took your clothes off.' Zafir's voice sounded cold and austere, and the look on his face was one of disgust.

Kat threw her napkin down and stood up, emotion making her voice shake. 'I am not here to be judged and condemned by you for a second time, Zafir. What I did, I did because I had no other choice. And it didn't do much good anyway, because the day before she was due to go to the facility my mother managed to do what she'd been trying to do for years—she successfully overdosed herself to death.'

Kat left the restaurant, weaving unsteadily through the tables, desperately trying to stem the onset of tears. Once out in the street, she hugged her arms around herself, suddenly cold. The bodyguards were alert, watching her from their car nearby. Noor didn't seem to be with them this evening, and Kat almost missed the other woman's presence.

She started to walk in the other direction, cursing her leg for a moment because she couldn't just run. The street was cobblestoned, and any uneven surface was treacherous for her now.

She heard steps close behind her and tensed, but then she felt something big and warm land on her shoulders and turned around to see a grim-looking Zafir holding her jacket and bag. He'd given her his coat.

She would have reached for her things, but she was afraid her hands would shake, so she clutched Zafir's coat around her, hating the fact that it felt so comforting and smelled so enticingly of him.

'I'm sorry,' he said abruptly.

Stunned by his apology, Kat responded unevenly, 'I… it's okay.'

Zafir ran a hand through his hair, his grim look being replaced by something close to anger. 'Dammit, Kat, if I'd known what had happened to you…why you were in that position…' He trailed off.

Old injury resurfaced and Kat said, 'You believed I didn't tell you because I was afraid you wouldn't marry me. That wasn't the reason at all, Zafir. I didn't tell you because I was ashamed of the choice I'd had to make. And because my world was so far removed from yours.'

'I might have at least been able to understand, though…'

Disgust crossed his face again, but this time Kat recognised it wasn't directed at her.

'That man took advantage of you when you were at your most vulnerable.'

She shook her head. 'He didn't take advantage of me,

Zafir. I made a choice to take up his job offer and earned a lot more money than I would have through a more traditional route. I have to take responsibility for that.'

Kat thought of telling Zafir everything—how the photographer had gone on to blackmail her once she'd become well-known—but something stopped her. It was an unwillingness to let him see just how far-reaching that bad choice had been, sending poisonous tendrils into her life for a long time afterwards. Better to let Zafir believe she'd just been bad with money than utterly naive. Because she'd been naive where he'd been concerned too. And the last thing she wanted was for him to know that.

Zafir's car pulled up alongside them with a low, sleek purr. They didn't go back into the restaurant and Kat felt bad now for rushing out, wondering what Zafir's friend and business partner must think.

As they drove silently back through the Paris streets Kat realised that the evening—apart from that abrupt ending—had been very pleasant. More than pleasant.

She said now, before she could censor herself, 'I liked that restaurant. Why did we never go there before?'

Zafir's face was cast into shadow and his voice sounded rueful. 'I liked to show you off...and, to be honest, I didn't think it was your scene.'

Kat fell silent, realising that she'd been so busy trying to live up to what she believed to be Zafir's high expectations of glamour and sophistication that she'd presented a largely false persona the whole time they'd been together.

Just before they reached the hotel, Zafir turned to her and asked, 'What was his name, Kat?'

Confused for a moment, she said, 'Who?'

'The man who took those pictures.'

Kat was shocked at the steel in Zafir's voice. She shook her head. 'It won't make any difference now—'

'Kat.' He cut her off. 'Either you tell me now or I'll find out my own way. All you'll be doing is saving my team some unnecessary work.'

She looked at him and knew it would be futile to deny Zafir when he was like this. 'What are you going to do?'

His mouth tightened. 'His name, Kat.'

Realising he'd only find out eventually anyway, she told him.

Satisfaction gleamed in Zafir's eyes as he got out of the car and came round to help her out. His hand was tight on hers, and he didn't let her go all the way up in the elevator and until he walked her to her door.

Her heart was thudding against her breastbone. She still had Zafir's coat around her shoulders and she shrugged it off now, handing it back. He took it, handing her her things.

Reluctant to look into those grey eyes, because it felt as if something fundamental had shifted between them and she wasn't sure where she stood any more, Kat turned to the door, inserting her key. It clicked and she pushed it open. She turned back at the last moment and forced herself to look at Zafir. His face was expressionless, but something burned deep in his eyes. Something that scared her as much as it excited her.

Her hand tightened on the door handle. 'Good night, Zafir.'

For a heart-stopping moment she thought he was about to step forward and kiss her, and she knew that if he did that she wouldn't be able to resist. She felt as if an outer layer of protective skin had been removed.

But Zafir just took a step back and said, 'Good night, Kat. Get some rest.'

Kat watched him leave, and a minute later she was still rooted to the spot and trembling all over. That explicit look had been hot enough to make her feel scorched all over. And hot enough to confuse the hell out of her. Because he'd walked away again.

She was also still reeling from his sincere apology. And his anger on her behalf at the photographer. He still didn't know the half of it. About the blackmail...

An insidious though sneaked into her head... Maybe she'd finally done it. Maybe the truth of her past had been enough to drive him away.

Realising she was still standing outside her room, Kat quickly went inside and rested her back against the door, doing her best to ignore her thumping pulse and the betraying feeling of disappointment.

But it was clear now: her past was a passion-killer. Zafir might still be attracted to her, but he didn't really want the whole unvarnished truth of her past getting in the way. She told herself that she should be happy. Relieved. This is what she wanted, wasn't it? To prove to herself that Zafir only wanted the superficial and nothing deeper.

But she wasn't happy—or relieved. She was in more turmoil than ever.

A short while later, in his own suite, Zafir paced up and down, his head reeling with what Kat had told him.

He knew he wouldn't be able to rest until he'd started a search for the man who had taken such advantage of her. Despite her insistence that she had been just as responsible.

Zafir had had no idea how erroneous those salacious newspaper reports had been, or how cruel. And when he thought of a much younger Kat, in dire straits, needing help, he felt a helpless raw fury rise up within him.

She hadn't kept all this from him for fear he'd break the engagement and because she'd sought financial security—it had been because she hadn't trusted him enough to accept her past. And she'd been right.

Recrimination blasted him. He'd judged and condemned her before she'd had a chance to say anything.

There was so much more to her than he'd ever given her credit for, and this insight was proving yet again that something he'd thought would be easy—seducing Kat into his bed again—was anything but. And yet he'd never wanted her more.

When Zafir met Kat at the door of her room, early the following evening, he stopped in his tracks. For a heart-stopping, pulse-pounding moment he thought she was naked. But then he realised that she was wearing a flesh-coloured dress that moulded to her every curve, dip and hollow. It had a high neck and long sleeves, so she was effectively covered up, and yet he'd never seen anything more provocative.

Her hair was up again, and she already wore the diamond. It sat, glittering, over the dress against her breastbone. Only the presence of the stylist and Noor and her guards stopped Zafir from overreacting and sending Kat back into her suite to change into a sack that would cover her from head to toe.

He was the one, after all, who had specified a wardrobe of clothes designed to show off the diamond to best advantage, and this dress did it perfectly. The problem was that it set Kat off to best advantage too, and the truth was that once again she effortlessly outshone the rare stone.

His eyes met hers and something clenched tight inside him when he saw a hint of vulnerability before she quickly masked it.

Willing the heat in his body down to a dull roar, he held out his arm to her and said, 'Shall we?'

* * *

The function was taking place in a ballroom at the very top of the hotel in which they were staying. It was sumptuous and decadent—and a blur to Kat. As was the view of Paris visible through open French doors on this unseasonably warm autumn evening. Apparently the rolling bank of clouds on the horizon heralded a storm, and Kat didn't appreciate the irony that the weather was mirroring her feelings so accurately.

She'd barely slept a wink last night, tossing and turning, wondering if she *had* driven Zafir away. As dawn had risen she'd felt gritty-eyed and hollow. Fully expecting that the next time she saw Zafir he would be looking at her with pity, or a kind of cool reserve.

But he hadn't. He'd looked at her with explicit heat in his eyes. And now she hated him for doing this to her, making her feel so confused and on edge.

Compounding her inner storm was the fact that Zafir had barely left her side. He was touching her constantly, either taking her arm or her hand, or placing his hand low on her back, just above her buttocks. She was hot all over and between her legs there was a merciless throb. Her breasts felt full and heavy, her nipples pressing against the material of the dress, but thankfully not glaringly obvious under the heavy material of the gown.

He'd turned away from her for a brief moment, and she was relishing the chance to get her breath and try to bring her heart rate under control again. But just as she was relaxing slightly a vaguely familiar voice called out.

'Kat! It's really you!'

Kat turned and a jolt of pure shock ran through her to see one of the only models she'd been relatively close with.

Her old friend stepped forward and enveloped Kat

in a huge hug. When she pulled back Kat saw the body-guards hovering protectively and said faintly, 'It's fine... I know her...'

She looked back at her friend and to her horror felt emotion threaten as remorse gripped her. Remorse for cutting her friend off after the accident. Cassidy had tried to contact her on numerous occasions, but Kat hadn't been capable of talking to anyone.

'I'm so sorry, Cass... I should have been in touch...'

Her friend took her hand and shook her head, 'No, Kat, you don't have to say anything. It's enough to see you now...' The stunningly beautiful Irish model, with her dark red hair, pale skin and blue eyes, smiled crookedly, 'But, *God*, I've missed you on the circuit.'

Kat smiled back, squeezing her friend's hand, appre-ciating this acceptance of her behaviour. She knew it was down to Zafir that her emotions were closer to the sur-face than usual, but that didn't help much.

Far too belatedly she spotted a tall, imposing man at her friend's side. He was dark and stern-looking, with compelling dark brown eyes. He also looked vaguely fa-miliar... It was only when Zafir stepped up to Kat's side again that she saw it—a distinct resemblance.

She also noted how this man slid his arm possessively around her friend's waist. Clearly they were lovers. He was looking at Kat's necklace and said in a deep and slightly accented voice, 'So this is the famous Heart of Jandor?'

Kat resisted the urge to touch the stone. 'Yes, it is.'

Then Zafir surprised her by saying, 'Welcome, Riad. Kat, this is my very distant cousin, Riad Arnaud, a de-scendant of my French great-grandmother who was gifted this very diamond. And this is Kat Winters, who I'm sure needs no introduction.'

Riad inclined his head towards Kat, and then he drawled, 'Some might say I have a claim on this diamond.'

Zafir responded, sounding unperturbed. 'It belongs to Jandor—as you very well know. Left to us by your ancestor.'

Zafir's cousin looked as if he was considering this, but then he smiled and his face was transformed from stern to gorgeous. The tension dissipated as he clapped Zafir on his shoulder and said, 'You do know how I like to wind you up about the diamond, and it never fails.'

Zafir let out a short laugh. 'It's good to see you, Riad. It's been far too long.'

Kat turned to Zafir then, and said, 'This is Cassidy O'Connor—an old friend of mine. We modelled together.'

Cassidy stepped out of Riad's embrace to shake Zafir's hand. Kat noted with interest how Riad's face tightened as he watched the two greet each other. There was something very proprietorial in his dark gaze and he quickly drew Cassidy back to his side. For a moment Kat felt a twinge of envy.

Riad was saying something about arranging a meeting and stepping back, but Kat's friend stepped forward to hug her again. She whispered into Kat's ear, 'Is everything okay? You look great, but…different.'

Kat pulled back and smiled weakly. 'I have a lot to tell you, Cass. I'll call you when I get home?'

Cass took her hand and squeezed it. 'Promise me you will. I don't want to lose touch again.'

Kat nodded and said, 'Promise.' Then she added impulsively, 'And you, Cass, are you okay? Are you both…?' She trailed off ineffectually.

To her surprise her friend paled slightly, but then she smiled brightly and said, 'I'm fine. And we…well, I'm not quite sure what we are, to be honest.'

And then her friend was gone, sucked back into the crowd with her brooding and enigmatic lover by her side, leaving Kat pondering that perhaps all was not as straightforward as it had seemed between them.

A while later, after a seemingly endless round of being introduced to people and being stared at, Kat's nerves were on end and she felt close to breaking point—physically and emotionally.

As if sensing her vulnerability, Zafir took advantage of a moment when they were alone and bent down to say, sotto voce, 'It's going to happen, Kat. Tonight.'

Those words…said with such implacable arrogance after his mixed messages pushed Kat over the edge of her control. She hissed up at him. 'No, it's not, Zafir. It's really not.'

She walked away as steadily as she could and felt his gaze boring into her from behind. She went through the open French doors and breathed in deep, hoping the cool air would calm her down.

Dark storm clouds were gathering on the horizon and she heard a distant crack of thunder. She was aware of someone hovering nearby—a bodyguard. And now she felt foolish for stalking off.

She wished in that moment that Zafir had never reappeared in her life. And then the thought of that made her suck in a pained breath and put a hand to her belly as if someone had just punched her.

Taking another deep breath, and assuring herself that she still had everything under control, Kat turned around and walked back into the room—only to see Zafir smiling indulgently down into the upturned face of a famous French actress, a renowned beauty, who had her scarlet-tipped nails firmly on Zafir's arm as she told him something undoubtedly scintillating and hilarious.

As if feeling the weight of her gaze, Zafir turned his head for a second and looked straight at her, with no expression on his face, and then he deliberately turned his back on her and his attention to the other woman.

The speed with which Kat became engulfed in a red mist of jealousy shocked her. As did the speed with which she could already imagine that Zafir had decided she was too much trouble to pursue, and was now turning to an easier and far more accommodating prospect.

Kat had made Zafir wait before finally agreeing to date him that first time. He'd been too overwhelming... intimidating. But a woman like that wouldn't make him wait. He'd give and she'd take and then move on...not like Kat, who'd never really moved on.

She turned away from the sight just as Rahul passed close by. Kat caught his arm impulsively. 'I've got a headache—do you think it'd be okay if I left now?' She crossed her fingers at the white lie.

Rahul immediately looked concerned and anxious. 'Let me just check...'

He was gone before she could stop him, and suddenly Kat couldn't bear to watch Zafir's face change expression as he was told that she wanted to leave early. She threaded her way through the crowd to where another of Noor's men was waiting and told him she was ready to give the necklace back. He looked unsure, but took her aside to a secure area and waited as she removed it and handed it over.

He and his colleague had it boxed up and whisked away within seconds. Discreet and efficient.

When Kat stepped back into the room she let out a sigh of relief that she couldn't see Zafir or Rahul. She pressed the button for the elevator, wanting to get out of Zafir's orbit before she made a complete fool of herself.

It finally arrived with a soft *ping* and the doors opened. She'd stepped in, and had just pressed the button to go down when a hand inserted itself into the closing doors, forcing them open again.

Zafir.

CHAPTER SIX

ZAFIR WAS ANGRY. 'Leaving so soon?'

Kat forced herself to sound cool. 'I have a headache.' She wasn't even lying now. She could feel a throbbing at her temples.

He frowned and stepped into the elevator with her as the doors closed. Instantly the space was dwarfed by his tall and broad masculine form. 'I'll see you down to your room.'

Panic surged. 'You don't have to—you shouldn't leave the function.'

Zafir shrugged even as his eyes stayed on her, alert. 'They'll hardly notice now, the champagne and cocktails have been flowing for a couple of hours. The object of the evening has been achieved. Jandor will be indelibly imprinted on their minds, thanks to you and the diamond.'

Zafir pressed the button and the elevator started moving with a little jolt. It was enough to make Kat sway and go off balance, falling backwards. As quick as lightning Zafir reached for her, taking her arms and hauling her against him.

They both sucked in a breath at the contact, and with a muttered curse Zafir reached out and slammed a hand on the stop button. Kat's hands were pressed against his chest as the elevator came to a juddering halt.

'What are you doing?'

'Do you really have a headache, Kat?'

She looked up at him helplessly. She knew if she tried to move he'd only pull her even closer, and as it was she could feel every hard plane of his chest, and down lower the unmistakable thrust of something much more potent. His arousal. For her? Or for that woman?

Heat and self-disgust flooded her body. She pushed herself away, stepping back until she hit the wall and could go no further.

Zafir took a step closer. 'You don't have a headache, do you?'

Kat bit her lip, but the sharp pain made no difference. Images of him laughing down at that woman, made her say rashly, 'What do you even care, Zafir? I'm just a living, breathing mannequin. Your guests will be missing your presence.'

Zafir's eyes flashed and then narrowed on her, and he came even closer. So close that she could see the beginnings of stubble along his hard jaw. The darker flecks of grey in those mesmerising eyes.

Softly he asked, 'You wouldn't be jealous, would you, Kat? Jealous that I was giving attention to a woman who made it obvious that she'd welcome me to her bed if I just said the word?'

Aghast that she'd exposed herself so easily and quickly, Kat blurted out, 'Don't be ridiculous. I don't care who you sleep with.'

Zafir stepped even closer. Close enough to touch. 'Liar,' he breathed. 'I think you do care.'

The expression on his face was fierce now. He put his hands on the wall, either side of her head, enclosing her with his whole body.

Kat was barely breathing. The tension was thick enough to cut with a knife. Her hands were balled into fists at her sides in an effort to stop herself from grabbing him—or smacking him.

'The truth is that you've reduced me to crude methods not even used by hapless teenage boys.'

Kat shook her head, finding it hard to focus. 'What are you talking about?'

Zafir's jaw clenched. 'I'm talking about making you jealous, Kat. I wanted to make you jealous. I wanted to provoke you into showing me something...anything...so that I don't feel as if I'm the only one going crazy here.'

Kat swallowed, all her turmoil dissolving and being replaced by a dangerous tenderness. She whispered unevenly, 'You're not going crazy...'

'The problem is,' he said, as if she hadn't spoken, his voice rough, 'that I *do* care who I sleep with, and unfortunately there's only one woman I want to sleep with. She's haunted me for months and I can't get her out of my head...not till I've tasted every inch of her again.'

Kat felt a dangerous languor steal over her. She was oblivious to the fact that they were in a stalled elevator. 'Who...?' she managed to croak out. 'Who is this woman?'

Zafir lowered his hands from beside her head and expertly wrapped one arm around her waist, pulling her into him. His other hand found and started plucking the pins from her hair as he said throatily, 'You know it's you, Kat...it's always been you.'

It's always been you...

Kat could feel tendrils of her hair falling down around her shoulders. She didn't have the strength to resist Zafir any more. She wanted him with an ache that was painful. And when his mouth touched hers she couldn't stop a helpless whimper of need escaping. Her hands were already unfurling and climbing up to wrap around his neck.

The kiss quickly became carnal and explicit. This was no gentle exploration. This was months of hunger and frustration. Months of X-rated dreams. Zafir demanded Kat's response and she gave it, arching her whole body into his as if they could just fuse there and then.

She was dizzy, ravenous for the taste of Zafir's mouth, sucking his tongue deep, nipping with her teeth. He was hot and hard against her belly, and she longed to wrap her hand around him and squeeze his flesh, remembering the way his breath would hiss between his teeth.

His hands roved over her back, slipping over her dress, feeling her curves. She felt constricted, her breasts pushing against the heavy fabric, nipples tingling with need.

Zafir's hands went lower, covering her buttocks, squeezing with his big hands, pulling her dress up. It was the sensation of air on her bare leg that finally managed to cut through the heated haze in Kat's brain, and with a stark feeling of sheer panic and dread she realised that Zafir was about to expose her in more ways than one.

She broke away from his kiss and opened her eyes. It took a second for her to focus, and her breathing was as jagged as her heart rate. The fact that Zafir looked similarly dishevelled was no consolation.

She'd almost forgotten...

She stepped to the side, her dress falling down around her legs. Covering her again. Her mouth felt swollen. Other parts of her felt sensitive. Slick. *God.* He'd been moments away from lifting her up so she could wrap her legs around his waist.

'What is it, Kat?'

She couldn't look at him. Her hair was half up, half down, and she raised trembling hands, trying to repair the damage. 'Please...just take me back to my room.'

For a long moment there was only the sound of harsh breathing in the small space, and then Zafir turned away and pressed a button. The elevator started moving again, and this time Kat put a hand on the wall to steady herself. She saw her clutch bag on the floor, where she must have dropped it, and bent down to pick it up with nerveless fingers.

Zafir's back was impossibly broad and remote in front of her. She longed to say something. Anything. But her tongue was frozen.

When the elevator doors opened Zafir stepped out. Kat followed him down the corridor to her room. She opened her clutch to get her key, but her hand was shaking too much to put it in the door. Any hope of disguising his effect on her was well and truly gone.

Her key was plucked out of her hand by a much bigger one and Zafir opened the door efficiently, waiting for her to go in. Kat wanted to sag down into a chair and take the weight off her quivering legs, but Zafir followed her in, closing the door behind him.

She faced him, heart thumping. 'Zafir, I didn't mean for you to—'

'Continue what we just started?' he inserted harshly.

He folded his arms. He'd never looked more formidable or gorgeous.

'Well, tough,' he said. 'Because I have every intention of finishing what we started.'

Kat shook her head and forced herself to speak as calmly as possible. 'I'm sorry, Zafir, if I gave you the impression...'

But the words dried up in her throat under his quelling look. She knew Zafir was more sophisticated than that. Just because they'd kissed, he wouldn't expect more now. But it wasn't about that. She'd felt the conflagration between them. It was unique. Unprecedented. Undeniable.

He unlocked his arms and shed his jacket, tossing it on a nearby chair. Then he reached for his bow tie and undid it with jerky moves, yanking open his top button.

He looked around. 'Do you have anything to drink in here?'

Kat lifted her hand and pointed to the drinks tray on a table near the window. Zafir strode over, more animal than man. He poured himself a shot of something and drank it back in one.

Then he looked at her. 'Do you want anything?'

Kat was shocked. It was as if a layer of civility had been stripped away. She'd never seen him like this. Not even that night when her world had crumbled to pieces around her.

She shook her head, even though her mouth was dry. 'No, I'm fine.'

Zafir slugged back another shot and turned around to face her. 'You're not, though, are you?'

Kat could feel herself pale.

How did he know?

'What do you mean?'

'What I mean is that for some reason you're determined to deny us this closure.'

Relief warred with anger.

He didn't know.

'You're so certain that resuming our physical relationship will end with everything neatly tied up in a bow?'

Hurt lanced her that Zafir could believe it would be so simple. But it would be…for him. Because he had no feelings involved. Only lust. She wished it could be so easy for her.

His mouth was a tight line. 'It's inevitable, Kat. We can't be within two feet of each other without going up in flames. Can you handle another week of this? Because I know I can't.'

One week. Surely she could survive one more week and then walk away, heart and soul still intact?

She lifted her chin. 'I can, Zafir. I'm sorry for what just happened…' A sudden flash of their two bodies welded together and how good it had felt to have him kiss her made her falter, but then she regained her composure and said, 'But it was a mistake.'

'A word I've heard more times than I care for lately,' Zafir said.

He started to pace then, and that only drew Kat's hungry eyes to his lean form.

He stopped suddenly to look at her. 'What is it, Kat? Is this punishment for what happened before? This is your retribution? Because I didn't give you a chance to explain your past? Because I judged you too harshly?'

Kat's eyes widened. It was so much more than that. That had been just the tip of the iceberg.

He hadn't loved her.

She backed away. '*No*, Zafir. I'm not that petty.'

She whirled away from him, afraid he'd see something of the emotion she was feeling on her face.

A bleak, futile anger rose up and she turned around again. 'It's not all about you, you know. There are things…things you don't understand.'

He frowned, and then his gaze moved over Kat's shoulder to something behind her and he frowned even harder.

She only had the barest moment of premonition before he said, 'Why are there crutches in your room?'

Kat wanted to close her eyes. She wanted to be on her own so she could curl up in a ball and pretend she'd never seen Zafir again. Pretend that her body wasn't pulsating with awareness just to be near him.

This was the moment of truth. It had been spectacularly naive or stupid of her to believe that she could keep her secret from Zafir. It was amazing that he hadn't found out already. And she'd never been less ready to tell him. Especially not after that moment in the elevator, reminding her of just how explosive it had always been between them. And how it could never be again. Not after this.

'Kat?' There was something stark in his voice. 'Who do the crutches belong to?'

She looked at him and swallowed painfully. 'Me. Because I need them.'

Zafir shook his head. Not understanding. And why would he?

'Tell me why you need them when you're standing in front of me right now.' He sounded harsh now.

It was time to stop hiding. Kat reached down and caught her dress in one hand. She pulled it up, revealing her prosthetic limb and the joint where it met her leg.

Even so, it took a few seconds for Zafir to understand what he was looking at—and when it finally registered he went pale. Eventually his gaze lifted back to her face. The room was so silent it felt like time had stopped.

'What are you showing me?' Zafir's voice was hoarse.

The dress fell from nerveless fingers to cover her leg again. She started to tremble and felt cold. She was going into shock. 'The accident…the one I mentioned. It was worse than I let you believe. They had to amputate… My foot…was crushed.'

She must have swayed or something, because suddenly Zafir was there, hands on her shoulders, pushing her down into a chair. He disappeared for a moment and then reappeared with a glass in his hand.

He held it up to her mouth. 'Drink some of this.'

Kat's eyes were on his as she lifted shaking hands to the glass and tipped back her head. The liquid burned down her throat and she coughed. Zafir took the glass away as fire bloomed in her chest, having an almost immediate effect on the numb coldness that had gripped her.

He put down the glass. His hands were on the chair's armrests either side of her. He looked as if he'd just been punched in the gut.

'Why didn't you tell me?'

Because I was using it as a crude defence to resist you.

Kat opened her mouth and shut it again uselessly, before saying finally, 'At first I didn't see that it was any of your business. And then...when you offered all that money to do the job... I couldn't afford to say no and I was afraid if you knew you'd think I couldn't do it.'

Zafir's grey gaze bored all the way through her. 'I don't think that's it at all—or not all of it.'

Feeling threatened, and horribly exposed, Kat pushed herself up out of the chair, forcing Zafir to stand. She stalked away from him, acutely aware of her limp now.

She whirled back, the truth spilling out. 'I'm different now, Zafir. You want the Kat I was before, and she doesn't exist any more. I didn't want to see you look at me the way others do—with horror and pity.'

She'd dreaded this moment ever materialising, and she feared that she'd avoided it for so long for the most basic reasons of vanity more than anything more noble. And that killed her when she knew she was so much stronger than that. But standing here now, in front of the only man who'd ever made her feel truly alive, she couldn't bear it. Tears weren't far away, and that would be the worst humiliation.

'You know where the door is, Zafir. Please, just go.'

But he didn't go. He came closer, and Kat held herself rigid for fear she'd shatter into a million pieces before she was alone again, when she could lick her wounds without that devastating gaze on her.

When Zafir spoke, he sounded harsh. 'You really think I hadn't realised that you'd changed in some very fundamental way? Have you not noticed that if anything it's only made me want you more?'

Kat blinked. She'd expected to be looking at a retreating back and a closing door. Not listening to Zafir sounding almost...hurt.

'You really think I'm that shallow?' he asked.

She might have before, when he'd more or less admitted he'd only proposed because she embodied some physical ideal, but now everything she'd thought she'd known about this man was jumbled up and contradictory.

She couldn't speak. The fact that he was still here was too much. The tears she was desperately holding back filled her eyes. She heard a curse, and then Zafir's white shirt became a blur in her vision as she was enveloped in strong arms and held tight against his body.

It was heaven and hell as a storm took hold of Kat that she had no control over and no choice but to give in to it. She wept for everything: her heartbreak, the loss of her leg, for her deceased and damaged mother and for the fact that she'd longed for Zafir's arms around her so many times...even though she'd denied it to herself.

For a long time she stood in the harbour of Zafir's arms as his hands moved soothingly over her back. *Compassion.* Another facet to this man she hadn't seen before, adding to the complexity she felt around him now.

When her sobs had finally died away she pulled back and looked with horror at Zafir's wet shirt. She could see the darkness of his skin underneath, and despite her paroxysm of emotion she felt awareness sizzle deep inside. Mortified—because any desire Zafir had ever felt for her must have been incinerated by now—she pulled herself free of his arms completely, wiping the backs of her hands across her hot, wet cheeks.

He was the last person in whose arms she'd expected to find solace. Her eyes felt swollen. She must have rivers of mascara down her cheeks. This truly was her lowest moment. And that was saying a lot, considering what she'd been through.

'I'm sorry,' she said thickly, avoiding his eyes, 'I don't know what came over me.'

He took her by the hand and led her over to a chair, pushing her down gently. He reappeared with a tissue, and another shot of alcohol in a glass. He crouched down before her and made her take a sip of the drink, until gradually she felt seminormal again.

He dipped another tissue in a glass of water and gently rubbed at her cheeks.

She was mortified at the emotional storm she'd just unleashed all over him—and at the way he was tending to her so easily.

When he'd put the tissue down she forced herself to look up from his damp shirt to his face, which was tense and unreadable. 'Your shirt is ruined.'

His mouth tightened. 'I couldn't care less about my shirt. In fact—' He broke off and stood up, starting to undo his buttons.

Kat's mouth opened as his impressive chest was revealed, bit by bit. 'What are you doing?' she squeaked, holding the glass to her like some sort of shield.

Zafir's shirt was open now, and he made short work of the cufflinks, throwing them on a nearby table before he let the shirt drop to the ground and then he knelt down in front of her again.

His naked and very masculine chest filled her vision. It was deliciously broad, with dark hair dusting defined muscles. And dark, flat nipples that she remembered were sensitive to the touch, earning her a hiss through his teeth whenever she'd lavished attention on them...

She felt bewildered and exposed. 'Zafir—'

'I want to see it, Kat. Show me your leg.'

Her insides clenched hard in rejection of that. But he looked determined. 'Why would you want to see it?'

Zafir couldn't exactly articulate why he needed to see Kat's leg, but it came from a visceral place deep within him that was boiling over with a mixture of volatile emotions. Reverberating shock, futile anger, and a kind of grief he'd only ever felt before for his sister.

'I want to see what happened to you.'

He could see the myriad expressions crossing her face, dominated by clear reluctance, and it made him want to go out and smash whoever had done this to her into tiny pieces. But then something else crossed her face that he couldn't decipher—something like resignation—and she put her hands on her dress, pulling it up over her knees.

The sparkling folds of the dress were gathered on her smooth thighs and he could see now where thick material like a sock came halfway up the thigh of her left leg. It was flesh-coloured. So it wouldn't be too noticeable? That sent another spurt of raw emotion through Zafir.

He moved back to give Kat room, watching as she pressed a button at the bottom of the prosthetic limb and then she pushed at it firmly, so that the whole apparatus slid down and off.

He absorbed fresh shock seeing her amputated leg, which now ended just a few inches below her knee. The thick, sock-like liner stretched from above her knee, to the bottom of her limb, where it was rounded and had a pin, which obviously slotted into the prosthetic leg to help keep it in place.

Her hands moved to the liner covering her leg and he could see that they were trembling. He moved forward and covered her hands, forcing her to meet his gaze by sheer will.

When she eventually looked at him he said, 'Let me?'

She bit her lip, and it looked so painful that Zafir wanted to reach out and rescue it, but then she said hoarsely, 'You don't have to do this.'

He reminded her, with an arrogance that felt hollow now, 'I don't have to do anything.' There was a heavy weight in his chest, an ache he'd never felt before.

Eventually she lifted her hands from under his and Zafir looked down and took a breath before carefully rolling the liner down Kat's thigh, over her knee and off, taking in the enormity of the moment as her naked leg was revealed.

He put both hands on her leg, cupping it, feeling the skin where it was so brutally cut short. The scar was a jagged but neat line, and he ached even harder to imagine the pain she must have gone through. The weeks and months of rehabilitation. The fact that he hadn't noticed anything before now was testament to her sheer will.

The earth could have stopped revolving outside, he was so focused on Kat and this moment. He looked at her. 'Tell me what happened?'

Her hands were tightly clasped in her lap, knuckles white. Her face was pale, eyes huge. 'It was dark. I was crossing a road... There was a truck and a motorcycle. They told me afterwards that the truck's brakes failed and it went out of control, hitting the motorcycle. I ended up in the middle. My foot...was crushed.'

Zafir thought of her broken, lying still on the road, and felt a dizzying surge of panic. It took him a moment to compose himself, but then he said, 'I'm so sorry, Kat... that this happened to you.'

She half shrugged, as if it was no big deal, but he could see the vulnerability in her eyes.

'The man on the motorcycle died, Zafir. He was only twenty-two. When you consider that... I was lucky.'

For a second Zafir's mind blanked as he thought of how easily it might have been Kat who had lost her life.

Bitterly he said, 'It sounds like the truck driver was the lucky one.'

Kat shook her head. 'He has to live with the guilt he feels every day. He came to visit me and I've never seen anyone so haunted.'

Zafir was humbled by her compassion. He realised now where her new steely strength came from, and he felt something like awe. He also felt a very sharp pang at the assertion that he should have been there for her.

But he hadn't—because he'd judged her on the basis of lurid headlines without really giving her a chance to explain her side. For the first time, Zafir felt a rush of remorse and regret. Everything had changed and yet, conversely, nothing had changed.

Kat felt so delicate and vulnerable under his hands, and yet strong. It made his blood pulse faster through his veins. Acting on pure instinct and need, Zafir spread his hands out, encompassing Kat's leg completely. He bent forward and pressed a kiss to her knee, then lower, to the top of her shin, his hands moving down and cupping her residual limb.

He heard her sucked-in breath and a strangled-sounding, 'What are you doing?'

He lifted his head and looked at her with explicit intention. He moved both hands up her leg at the same time, until they encircled her bare thigh. Blood thundered in his veins.

'What do you think I'm doing, Kat? I'm finishing what we started.'

CHAPTER SEVEN

KAT COULDN'T BREATHE. Again. It was a miracle that any oxygen was reaching her brain. Somehow, from somewhere, she managed to suck in a breath. And another one. Her heart rate wouldn't slow, though. She felt flayed alive. Raw. But deep within her core burnt a fire that not even her turmoil could quench.

She'd expected Zafir to be long gone by now. But he wasn't. He was kneeling at her feet, looking up at her with that molten silver gaze. It was uncompromisingly direct, leaving her nowhere to hide.

And yet her mind reeled. He'd just looked at her... touched her leg. Inspected it. Cupped it reverently. Kissed it.

Emotion threatened again. The only people who'd touched her there since the accident had been medical professionals, or herself when she'd had the nerve to, and it had taken a long time to do it without crying.

Yet Zafir had just done it, and he hadn't looked remotely horrified or disgusted. He'd looked sad. Angry. Fierce. And there'd been something unmistakably possessive in his touch too—as if he was claiming some kind of ownership of her damaged limb. Which was obviously just a figment of her overwrought brain.

She shook her head, forcing herself to articulate her scattered thoughts. 'You don't mean that...'

Something struck her then, and she went cold all over. Zafir was a proud man. A very alpha man. A man full of integrity.

She recoiled back in the seat. 'You don't have to prove

anything, Zafir. If you stand up and walk away it won't make you less of a man.'

His hands tightened on her thigh and his eyes widened. A look of affront came over his hard-boned face. 'First you think I'm too shallow to handle this news and now you're accusing me of being too proud to walk away from something I don't want to do?'

Kat swallowed. She'd never seen Zafir look more stern.

His voice resonated deep within her. 'I would have thought that the least you know about me by now, Kat, is that I don't ever do anything I don't want to. I want something and I go after it. Do I need to remind you of how I went after you?'

She shook her head quickly. She did not need a reminder of that all-consuming seduction right now—her brain was addled enough as it was.

'I am here,' he said, 'because I want you, Kat. I tracked you down because I couldn't get you out of my head. Because I believe we have unfinished business. Because I believe that I won't be able to get on with my life until I've tasted you again…until I'm buried so deep inside you that I might finally be able to think clearly again. What happened to you changes nothing about how much I want you.'

All Kat heard was 'until I'm buried so deep inside you' and her whole lower body clenched, as if it was already anticipating taking his body into hers. As if some muscle memory was already reacting just to his words.

She clamped her thighs together, trapping Zafir's hand. His eyes flashed. He knew. He could sense her helpless response. But insecurity warred with desire. Did he really still want her?

With gentle but remorseless force, Zafir pushed her knees until they were spread apart and he was between them. Her dress was ruched up around her thighs, and if he looked he would see her very plain white panties.

As if reading her mind, his hands moved upwards, and Kat's breathing grew ragged and fast. Within seconds he would know just how badly she ached for him. She'd be utterly exposed.

She reached down and covered his hands, stopping their progress, and shifted, sitting up straighter in the chair, trying to put some space between them. She seized on something, *anything*, that might restore sanity, even though the blood rushing through her body wasn't asking for sanity at all. The opposite...

'I haven't been with anyone since—' She stopped. She'd been about to say *since you*, but she didn't want Zafir to know that. It would mean too much. She hoped he'd assume she'd meant to say *since the accident*.

Zafir shook his head. 'None of that matters. What matters is here and now.'

He rested his arms on the armrests of her chair and just looked at her. Her thighs were bracketing his chest...she could feel the tiny abrasions of his chest hair against the delicate skin of her inner thighs. Between her legs she was so damp and hot it was embarrassing.

'You're so beautiful,' he said simply.

Kat wanted to duck her head, avoid that blistering gaze, but she couldn't. She couldn't speak.

Zafir bent forward and touched his mouth to hers.

Kat closed her eyes and a helpless sound of need flowed from her mouth to his as the kiss hardened and deepened. It was too late for sanity. She couldn't resist this. *This* was what she wanted and needed to make all of the questions and doubts and insecurities fade away. When Zafir touched her she couldn't think of anything else. And she didn't want to.

On every level he'd defeated her. Kat's whole body

arched towards his, her arms finding and twining their way around his neck as his kiss got deeper and darker, and so explicit that it sent electric shocks all the way through her core, against which Zafir's taut belly provided a delicious friction.

His hands were on her thighs, lifting them up to hook around his hips. Kat didn't have time to think about how she looked, or how the lack of her limb felt. Zafir was too all-consuming.

One hand was on her back now, finding the top of the zip at her neck. He tugged it down and she felt air touch her bare skin as the dress slackened around her breasts. Zafir took his mouth off hers to pull back. They were both breathing harshly.

Without taking his eyes off hers, he pulled her dress forward and down, easing it off her shoulders and down her arms until she was naked from the waist up. The design of the dress had precluded the need for a bra.

Then he looked down at her.

She saw the way his eyes grew even darker, and colour slashed across his cheeks as he took in her bare breasts.

He said something guttural in Arabic. And then he brought his hands to her flesh, cupping her and squeezing. Her nipples were hard, stinging points, and when Zafir passed a thumb over each of them she almost cried out, they were so sensitive.

He looked at her and said raggedly, 'I've dreamt of this. Of you...'

He put one hand on her back, encouraging her to arch towards his mouth. He cupped her breast with his other hand, and then surrounded first one nipple and then the other in hot sucking heat. Kat's hands were buried in his hair, clinging on for dear life as he stoked her arousal to painful levels.

It was as if a wire was directly connecting Zafir's

mouth on her breasts to her core. The deliciously wicked combination of his rough tongue and teeth on her sensitive flesh pushed her right over an edge she didn't see coming, and she found herself shuddering in his arms as an orgasm gripped her and threw her high, before letting her float back down to earth.

She stiffened and pulled back in mortification, her cheeks burning. Her body had just betrayed her spectacularly. She shook her head. 'I'm sorry... I—'

He stopped her with a finger to her mouth. He looked wild. 'Don't you dare apologise. If I don't get inside you soon, Kat, I'm in danger of disgracing myself in a way that only used to happen when I was a boy and unable to control my body.'

Her eyes widened as comprehension sank in. 'You mean you—'

'Yes,' he said succinctly. And then, 'Where's the bedroom?'

All semblance of civility was gone now. And it was the sexiest thing Kat had ever seen.

'Behind you.'

With effortless strength, Zafir stood and scooped Kat up against his chest. Her arms went around his neck as he kicked open the bedroom door and brought her into the dimly lit room.

The gathering storm clouds outside went unnoticed as Zafir lowered Kat to the bed. So did the jagged fork of lightning and the first drops of heavy rain.

A part of Kat couldn't believe this was happening, and she needed a moment to assimilate everything and analyse the consequences. And yet, in spite of this knowledge, she couldn't bring herself to utter a word as she lay back and watched Zafir strip off the rest of his clothes with all the natural-born confidence of a spectacularly beautiful, sexually virile man.

Kat's eyes widened as she took in a sight she'd thought she'd never see again. A very aroused Zafir. Her greedy gaze avidly took in his whole body, noting that his muscles seemed even harder than before. His body bigger. And yet he was leaner. As if he'd shed some softer layer. Maybe becoming a King had done that to him.

'You, Kat,' he said gutturally. 'I want to see you too.'

He started to tug at her dress, pulling it down over her hips and off completely. Now she only wore her plain white panties, and she felt embarrassed. She'd always made an effort before, aware that Zafir had once liked wispy concoctions of lingerie—usually sent to her by him. But as he came down beside her on the bed now, his eyes gleamed with a hunger that turned any doubts to dust.

His hand smoothed over her chest and belly, which contracted with need. When his hand reached her underwear and his fingers slid underneath to explore she put a hand down instinctively. He looked at her. Once again she bit her lip. Unsure. As if she hadn't ever lain with this man before. As if he hadn't just seen her fall apart after barely touching her.

'I haven't… I don't look after myself down there like I used to.' Her cheeks burned.

Zafir's nostrils flared. 'Kat…when are you going to get it? *Nothing* about you could turn me off.'

His words unleashed a fresh flood of heat, and she realised now how careful she'd always been to live up to some ideal that she'd thought he wanted. His hand explored further, over the curls she'd always been told she had to remove for the sake of lingerie modelling contracts.

When his fingers touched her very core she arched her back off the bed. Within seconds her panties were gone and her legs were splayed. Zafir clamped big hands on her thighs, holding her captive as he bent his head and proceeded to explore her drenched sex with a thoroughness that rendered her insensible.

Her first orgasm had taken her by surprise. This one built and built until she almost screamed with the need to release the tension—and then Zafir circled her clitoris with his tongue, sucking it roughly, and she exploded into a million pieces.

When he loomed up over her he looked like a god. A dark, sexy, dangerous god. His muscles gleamed with sweat and she could smell his arousal—and hers. And even though her body wanted to float on a sea of bliss after that orgasm, when she heard the snap of latex and looked down to see Zafir's hands on his straining erection, need gripped her like a vice again. He made her insatiable. Greedy. She felt as if she'd been starved of some vital thing and was only now realising how empty she'd been.

He came down over her and aligned their bodies. She could see nothing else but him, feel nothing else but him. He surrounded her utterly.

After a breath he thrust into her body, deep and hard and unequivocal. As if stamping his brand on her. Kat breathed in the sheer expanse of him, awed at the way he filled her so completely. It was all at once familiar and altogether new. It was exquisite.

For a heart-pounding moment Zafir stayed embedded in her like that, as if he too was savouring the moment. And then something inside Kat broke apart. She reached for him, wrapping her arms around his neck, arching upwards. And as he started to move in long slow strokes in and out of her body's tight clasp, she gave herself over to the sensations racing through her body, rendering her mute.

His movements quickened and became less controlled,

he reached for her left thigh and brought it up, holding it firmly, deepening his penetration. Kat was only aware of the pinnacle of pleasure beckoning. It came at them like a steam train, blasting them apart and then welding them back together as Zafir's big body slumped over hers. They were so joined at every possible point, Kat wasn't sure she'd ever been a separate entity.

She fell into an exhausted slumber under Zafir's weight, unaware of him moving off her and standing up from the bed, looking at her as though he'd never seen her before.

Zafir was still reeling a few hours later as he looked out at the dawn breaking over the Paris skyline. The storm had passed—a storm he'd only been peripherally aware of. He felt as if a bigger storm had just happened in this hotel room.

In him.

He could see the shape of Kat on the bed in the reflection of the window, her elegant curves, her breasts…

He turned around and looked at her properly, his gaze inevitably tracking to her left leg, where it ended so cruelly short. He could see the faint imprint of his hand on the pale skin of her thigh, where he'd obviously gripped her in the throes of the most urgent lust that had ever gripped him.

As if hearing his thoughts, she moved minutely on the bed, and Zafir's chest tightened when he saw how her left leg instinctively wanted to stretch out. He wondered if she experienced the 'phantom limb' that people spoke of, when they could feel the pain of their amputated limb even though it wasn't there any more.

Seeing her like this… It made him feel so many different emotions he wasn't sure where one started and the other ended. But mostly he felt angry that she hadn't trusted him enough to tell him. And, worse, that she'd clearly expected him to turn tail and run.

But then, he had to concede heavily, why would she have thought otherwise? After all, he'd pursued her relentlessly after seeing her model lingerie on a catwalk. Why wouldn't she believe that he was shallow enough to value physical perfection over anything else?

He shook his head. Sex with Kat had always been amazing. So amazing that it had prompted him to track her down again. But this...what they'd just shared...had reached a whole new level. He didn't remember it ever being so carnal or so visceral. He'd literally had to have her...or die. Sinking into her that first time had impacted on him on a level where sex never usually did.

He went cold as the significance of that sank in. It had felt like coming home. But not in the way that returning to Jandor always felt like coming home... This had been far more profound and disturbing. It had felt like coming back to a place he'd longed for without even realising it.

Zafir's immediate reaction was to negate this revelation as a lust-induced delusion, but the truth was harder to deny.

Things with Kat had morphed out of all recognition. And it had nothing to do with the fact that she'd been hiding the truth that she was an amputee. It had everything to do with the fact that after having sex with this woman closure had never seemed more distant.

He dragged his gaze back up her body to her face. She was awake now, and looking at him with wide golden eyes. And just like that desire returned—urgent and swift.

Her gaze tracked down his body, obviously taking in his helpless physical reaction. Her cheeks coloured as she said in a sleepily husky voice, 'You showered...'

For a second Zafir warred with his emotions and tendrils of panic growing inside him. This was so far beyond what he'd expected to experience with Kat again that he wanted to tell her that last night had been enough. He wanted to walk out through the door and never look back. Because suddenly things weren't as simple as he'd thought they would be.

But that urge to leave curdled in his belly.

He didn't want to leave. He wanted her.

Compelled by a force stronger than he could deny, he twitched his towel off his hips and stalked back to the bed. He lay down alongside Kat and touched her thigh, seeing how something in her eyes veiled itself.

'I marked you...'

She looked down and saw his handprint. Her hair hid her face as she said in a slightly breathless voice, 'It's okay...it doesn't hurt.'

Zafir scooped her hair over her shoulder and tipped her chin up so she had to look at him. She was wary, but he could see the heat in her eyes. He kept his eyes on hers as he moved so that he was between her thighs... his erection notched against the place where she was hot and wet. Ready for him.

It was too much. Zafir didn't have a hope as he gave in to the raging desire inside him, blocked out all the warning voices and slid home. Again. And again. Until he was reduced to rubble and the voices were mercifully quiet.

Kat woke up surrounded by steel and heat. She couldn't breathe. Panic gripped her and she instinctively thrashed out, flailing uncontrollably.

She vaguely heard a sound, but it took long seconds for her to realise that Zafir had all but pinned her to the bed and was now looming over her saying, 'Kat, relax— it's me... You're okay.'

She went still, even though panic still raced through

her blood. Eventually it dissipated and she asked shakily, 'What happened?'

'You were lashing out…screaming. "Get it off me! Get it off…"'

The first tendrils of understanding sank in, quickly followed by embarrassment. She breathed deep. Zafir's very naked body was over hers, but even that couldn't distract her from the fact that she'd just had the same nightmare she'd had for months after the accident.

She pulled back from Zafir's embrace and he let her go reluctantly, as if he knew she needed space but didn't want to allow it.

She struggled to find a way to explain herself. 'I'm sorry… If I feel claustrophobic it brings back the accident…when I was trapped under the truck.'

Zafir reared back. 'I make you feel claustrophobic?'

Kat was shocked at the hurt she heard in Zafir's voice. '*No*…no. I'm just not used to waking up in bed with someone.'

Kat realised that part of it was disbelief that Zafir was still here—that she'd woken in his arms. The claustrophobia lingered, but it had nothing to do now with traumatic memories and everything to do with feelings rising inside her that she didn't want to analyse, like a coward.

She sat up and avoided his eye. 'I think I'll take a bath. Could you pass me my robe, please?'

Zafir said nothing for a long moment, and then he got out of the bed, unashamedly naked, and handed her a silken robe. Kat watched him walk into the bathroom and registered the sound of water running. She quickly pulled on the robe, covering her own nakedness, and scooted to the edge of the bed.

Zafir reappeared in the doorway, still naked. Ridiculously, Kat felt like blushing and she blurted out, 'Could you hand me my crutches?'

Zafir strode over, saying, 'You don't need your crutches.'

He was about to bend down and pick her up into his arms but Kat put out her hands, heart thumping treacherously at the innately masculine reaction.

'No, Zafir, I can do it myself.'

He drew back and looked down at her, a muscle pulsing in his jaw. 'Very well.'

He went and retrieved her crutches from the other room and Kat pulled herself upright on them, making her way into the bathroom, burning with self-consciousness. The only people who had seen her like this were medical professionals and Julie. Not a lover. Not Zafir.

She didn't want to turn around to see what might be on his face and she shut the bathroom door behind her, feeling alternately stronger than she'd ever felt but also weak. As if she'd scored some useless point.

She turned off the taps of the bath and disrobed, carefully stowing the crutches and lowering herself into the steaming, fragrant water.

The water lapped around her and a sense of déjà vu struck her as she recalled the last time she'd had a bath and where her mind had gone. She couldn't stop the images of the night they'd just shared from circling in her head like a lurid movie.

When he'd come back to the bed as dawn had broken they'd made love again. He'd pulled her over his body so that she was straddling him, and just before he'd thrust up into her body he'd asked, 'Is this okay? Are you comfortable?'

She'd nodded, aghast at how overcome she'd felt in that moment. She'd never seen this far more tender and gentle side to Zafir before. Even though there was nothing tender or gentle about their lovemaking.

She'd been so…uninhibited. Sex with Zafir had never felt like this. Before, she'd always felt somehow…aware of herself. Aware of all the women he'd been with before her and of her inexperience. It was as if a wall of glass had separated them, and no matter how skilful Zafir had been Kat had never lost herself completely, always holding some part of herself back.

But last night had been different. She'd lost herself completely. There'd been nothing between them but heat and lust and desperate need. It was as if she'd undergone some seismic shift.

There was a knock on the door, making her jerk upright. 'Kat, are you all right?'

Her voice sounded strangled as she called out, 'Fine. I'm fine.'

Zafir scowled on the other side of the door. Everything in him burned to go to her. He could imagine Kat's naked body all too well—slick and wet, droplets of water beading on her nipples...

He paced back and forth, aware of his body responding to his imagination. Cursing softly, he pulled a towel around his waist, as if that could douse his desire.

She'd looked so proud just now, walking into the bathroom on her crutches, back straight and tall. The stark reality of what she'd gone through had impacted on him all over again. It had almost but not quite eclipsed what he'd felt when she'd told him she felt claustrophobic. *Hurt.* An emotion he'd only ever felt around his siblings when they'd used to shut him out.

Hurt was not an emotion he welcomed. He'd always liked and respected Kat, but he'd never claimed to love her. He wanted no part of that—not after seeing his brother so destroyed by it.

Once again Zafir felt the urge to just walk away. Consign this to the status of a one-night stand. A slaking of lust. But even as he thought that he knew it was a lie. His body burned for her. One night would never be enough.

Just then there was the sound of splashing and a muffled curse. Zafir didn't even think. He walked straight into the bathroom.

Kat was sitting up in the bath and she looked at him. All he saw was gleaming pale skin and those glorious breasts rising from the water.

'I heard…something…' he said, feeling ridiculous.

'I just dropped the soap.'

Kat's cheeks were pink. Her hair was piled high, but long tendrils clung to her skin. Giving up the fight, Zafir muttered a curse and dropped the towel from around his hips, seeing Kat's eyes widen as she took in his helplessly rampant response.

Zafir was climbing into the bath before Kat could react. She squeaked as he settled himself behind her, making water slosh over the edge of the bath. 'What are you doing?'

His arms were around her, pulling her back against his broad chest, and the past and present meshed painfully for a moment, reminding of her of many such shared moments before.

'Zafir…' she protested weakly.

'Yes?' Zafir started to lather his hands with soap and then spread them over her body.

'You don't have to do this…' Kat tensed her body, trying to hold back the emotion she was feeling.

Zafir's hands stilled. He angled himself around to see her face. 'What is it?'

Kat shrugged, as if this wasn't a big deal. 'I just… This kind of thing has been so far from my mind… I certainly never expected that when the time came it would be you…'

Her heart beat fast. This was the closest she could come to trying to articulate the tangled feelings in her breast.

'And are you glad it's me?'

Kat knew now that she was in serious trouble, because experiencing this reawakening with him was more profound than she liked to admit. Not that she could tell him that. Not when to him this was just an affair to gain *closure*.

She shrugged again and said—as nonchalantly as she could when he was at her back, surrounding her in heat and desire, 'You're a good lover, Zafir...'

A good lover.

Zafir curbed his tongue. How did she manage to make that sound almost insulting? As for the thought that she would have let some other man see her for the first time as she was now... Zafir didn't even want to contemplate that scenario.

He concentrated instead on washing Kat's body with an explorative zeal that would soon make her admit that—*what?* What did he want her to admit? Zafir suddenly wasn't sure...

But then he felt Kat start to soften against him, her back arching against his chest, her body moving restlessly under the water, and as he found the slick centre of her body and made her moan he told himself he didn't care. *This* was all he cared about. Here and now.

It was enough. It would be enough.

CHAPTER EIGHT

SOME HOURS LATER Kat was dressed and ready to go, but she was delaying her exit from the bedroom to join Zafir in the suite, where he'd gone to make some calls, because the full significance of the previous night and everything that had happened was sinking in fully—and very belatedly. As if she'd been blocking it out until now.

Just thinking of Zafir's easy acceptance of her secret and how tender he'd been was overwhelming. At every step when she'd expected him to look at her in horror, turn and walk away…reject her…he'd done the opposite.

A flashback came of sweaty limbs entwined, his hand hard on her thigh, clamping her in place so he could thrust even deeper…

Kat felt a fine sweat break out over her body.

To say she was raw and exposed was an understatement. She hadn't felt like this since the aftermath of the accident. It was as if he'd torn her apart and put her back together, and now she wasn't sure who she was any more.

The thought of that grey gaze narrowing on her made her pace back and forth now, gnawing at a nail. A bad habit she'd cut out years before.

Zafir had effectively demolished every wall she'd erected around herself last night, and now there was nothing left to hide behind. The knowledge that she'd been using her leg as a defence mechanism to keep him at a distance was not welcome. And the thought of another night like last night was terrifying.

She was very much afraid he'd effortlessly expose things that she wasn't even ready to admit to herself yet. Like how far he'd burrowed under her skin again. Like how much she yearned for him to look at her as he had before, when she'd done no wrong in his eyes.

He'd used to look at her and say, 'I can't believe someone like you exists in this world…'

A curt rap on the door stopped Kat in her tracks.

'Kat? Are you ready? My car is waiting to take us to the airport.'

To take them to Jandor. Back to the place where Kat had realised just how ill-suited she was to become a permanent part of Zafir's life. And yet she'd tried to convince herself it would be all right.

Her recent thoughts and revelations still reverberating in her head sickeningly, she walked to the door and opened it. Zafir filled her vision. He'd changed into a charcoal suit and looked regal and impressive.

Before she could stop herself, she blurted out, 'There's something I need to say before we leave.'

Unfazed, even though Kat could imagine the veritable army of people waiting for them to leave, he just said, 'Okay.'

She was glad of her slim-fitting trousers and silk shirt. She wanted to send out a no-nonsense vibe.

She walked into the suite and turned around to face Zafir, steeling herself. 'What happened last night won't be happening again.'

Even as she said it she could feel her heart give a betraying lurch. And between her legs pulsed as if in protest.

Zafir leant his shoulder against the doorframe and folded his arms. He raised a brow. 'And why would that be?'

Kat wanted to pace, but forced herself to stand still and sound cool and blasé. 'Because last night was enough for me. And, in any case, Jandor is hardly an appropriate location for the King to be conducting an illicit affair with someone who is eminently unsuitable.'

Zafir straightened up from the wall, his gaze narrowing on her just as she'd feared. 'You never did like Jandor.'

Kat thought she detected a note of bitterness in his voice, and she responded defensively. 'That's *not* true. From the moment I first saw it from the plane I thought it was magical...'

Zafir looked sceptical.

'It's true,' Kat said, less vehemently now, afraid of revealing too much. 'I loved Jahor too. It was just... The palace was so huge and intimidating.'

She shivered now, remembering the massive empty corridors. The hushed reverence. Her fear of doing something wrong. The feeling of hundreds of eyes on her that she couldn't see.

'And you were so busy. I hardly saw you.' Kat hated the accusing note in her voice.

To her surprise, Zafir unfolded his arms and ran a hand through his hair.

He sighed. 'Maybe you're right. My father monopolised my attention.' Those grey eyes pinned her to the spot. 'I shouldn't have left you alone so much.'

Kat broke eye contact, not wanting him to see how much that impacted on her. 'It wouldn't have changed anything in the end,' she said. She had to keep reminding herself of that fact. If not him.

'I'm sorry I hurt you, Kat. I never meant to do that.'

Kat went very still. *This* was why they couldn't sleep together again. Zafir was getting far too close to the beating heart of her, and she didn't want him to suspect that that was why she couldn't repeat last night.

She looked at him and said, very deliberately, 'I was infatuated with you, Zafir. Not in love. It was for the best. I wasn't ready to step into such a hugely responsible role. I would have disappointed you. And, even though I know you would have been happy with a marriage based on respect and chemistry, it wouldn't have been enough for me in the end.'

She knew that much now—indelibly. She needed to be loved in a way that had eluded her all her life. For herself. Not just because she represented some ideal and as such could be used as a commodity, as her mother had used her so shamelessly. And as she had used herself when she'd had to.

An impulse rose from deep inside her at that moment, a desire to unsettle Zafir as much as he unsettled her. 'What about you, Zafir?' she asked before she could stop herself. 'Would a marriage in little more than name really have been enough for you? Are you so cold?'

Zafir was silent for a long moment, and then he said, almost harshly, 'Yes, I am that cold. I was brought up to rule a country, not to fall in love. My parents' marriage was borne out of a need to unite two warring countries. There was no love lost between them, and yet together they brought peace to a region. Surely that's more important than the selfish desires of one person to indulge in the myth of a fairy tale?'

Kat tried to hide her shock. 'I know things are different for you…that you're not the same as the average person…' *Not remotely*, said a little voice. 'But I don't think it's too much to ask, Zafir…even for you.'

He started to pace, and as much as Kat had wished to unsettle him, now she regretted it. He stopped and looked at her accusingly. 'Love tore my brother apart. Destroyed him.'

Kat put a hand on the back of a chair near to her, as if that might steady her. 'What do you mean?'

Zafir had never really talked about his younger brother before, but she knew he existed. He had a reputation as a debauched playboy, and from the photos she'd seen of him in passing, in the gossip pages, he was as tall, dark and handsome as his brother, with a roguish edge that had earned him a place as one of the world's most elusive bachelors.

Zafir said, 'I had a younger sister—Sara. She was Salim's twin. They were playing one day in a walled garden. They were messing about as usual…' Zafir lifted a hand and let it drop. 'I heard Salim scream and I ran to them. She was dead when I got there…a massive head injury… She'd fallen from the high wall…'

Kat wanted to go and touch Zafir as anguish filled her chest, but it was as if he was still surrounded by that wall. 'Oh, Zafir… I'm so sorry. How old was she?'

He looked bleak. 'Just eleven.'

He went over to a window and looked out, his back to Kat. She sat down in the chair.

'They were so close, the two of them. From the moment they were born they had their own little world. Even spoke a language no one else could decipher. When she died…and when Salim realised how little our parents had valued Sara because she'd been a girl and not a boy… something broke inside him.'

After a long moment Zafir turned around. He was expressionless.

'I saw what loving someone and losing them did to Salim. It changed him for ever. I have no intention of ever investing so much in one person that they have the power to destroy you.'

A million things crowded onto Kat's tongue. She wanted to say to Zafir that Salim and Sara had obviously had a very strong twin bond, and of course Salim had taken her death hard, but that was no reason to believe Zafir would experience the same thing. But Kat's tongue wouldn't work. She guessed that whatever she said would be met with deep cynicism.

She stood up and tried to ignore the tightness in her chest. 'I'm sorry you had to experience losing your sister like that, Zafir. I think I would have liked to know her...'

'Yes...' he said almost wistfully. 'I often wonder how she would be now. I think she would be formidable.'

No more formidable than her older brother, thought Kat.

There was a sharp rap on the door at that moment, and Kat flinched.

Rahul's anxious voice floated through the door. 'Sire, the cars are waiting.'

Zafir's gaze narrowed on Kat again as he called out, 'Just a minute.'

She felt a frisson of danger as he walked over to where she stood with all the inherent grace and menace of a predatory animal. Their recent conversation was forgotten as that grey gaze skewered her to the spot.

'You meant what you said? You're certain this affair ends here?'

For a heart-jolting moment Kat thought that Zafir might just leave her here in Paris and go on without her. Maybe she'd pushed him too far, asking those questions...

She forced herself to nod.

Zafir snaked a hand around the back of her neck, under her hair. She went on fire.

He shook his head. 'It's not over, Kat—not yet. You can delude yourself that it is, but when you're ready to be honest and admit that it's not I'll be waiting.'

The worst thing, as he stepped back and she struggled to find some pithy response, was the relief rushing through her that he wasn't leaving her behind.

Not yet.

* * *

The setting sun bathed Jahor in warm golden light. Kat couldn't believe how overwhelmed she was to be back here again, but she told herself it had nothing to do with learning about Zafir's sister and brother or her renewed intimacy with Zafir.

She'd once had a very real fantasy of becoming Queen of this land, humbled and awed by Zafir's belief in her, but that fantasy had been cruelly shattered. She felt it keenly now, though—the sense of loss—even though she knew that it was better this way.

She wouldn't have known the first thing about being Queen. She would have let Zafir down. And she went cold now, thinking of how much worse it would have been if her past had come out after she had become Queen.

Zafir was sitting beside her in the back of a chauffeur-driven car, speaking on his phone in a low, deep voice as they wound their way through the ancient streets and up to the palace on the hill, overlooking the ancient city.

She was glad his attention wasn't focused on her for this moment. During the flight from Paris she'd found his gaze resting on her every time she'd looked at him, and by the time they'd disembarked her senses had been jangling with awareness.

She just had to resist him. That was all.

She could see people through the tinted windows of the car, bowing reverently as they passed by. And then a gaggle of gap-toothed boys chased the car, waving manically even though she knew they couldn't see her or Zafir. She felt an impulse to open her window and reach out to touch their hands, and it shocked her.

It was another reminder of how she'd never have had the decorum to be Queen. So why didn't that thought comfort her? Why did it leave her feeling hollow?

They were sweeping through the palace gates now, and

into the majestic forecourt. Nerves fluttered in Kat's belly as Zafir ended his phone call and said enigmatically, 'You might find some things a little changed since last time.'

When she got out of the car she could see several aides waiting, and Rahul, looking as efficient as ever. Staff greeted them, dressed in long, light-coloured tunics and close-fitting trousers. They were smiling as they took her luggage and Zafir's.

The last time she'd been there the staff had been dressed in black, and they'd had a dour air. There'd also been an oppressive atmosphere, but now there was an air of infectious joyousness.

A smiling young woman came forward to greet Kat, saying in perfect English, 'I'm Jasmine. I'll be your maid while you're here, Miss Winters. If you'd like to follow me?'

Kat looked over to where Zafir was still watching her, and he said, 'Go—settle in and rest. I'll come and find you.'

Then he was striding away, his aides and Rahul hurrying in his wake. And, in spite of Kat's intentions to put some distance between herself and Zafir, all she felt right then was bereft. But, she told herself sternly, that this was a good thing if it reminded her of how out of place she'd felt here before. It would help her to resist Zafir.

She was led over to a nearby golf buggy and the younger woman indicated for Kat to get in. Kat did so, and soaked up the glorious lingering heat and the beautifully cultivated gardens as Jasmine carefully drove them round to where Kat's suite was located, at the other side of the palace.

On her first visit, Kat remembered walking miles and miles through vast corridors behind a silent woman as she'd been led to her quarters, feeling as though she was being punished for something she hadn't done.

Her rooms were different this time—which she was grateful for. She had enough memories bombarding her brain without adding more to the mix. Memories of long hot nights when Zafir had crept into her bed and woken her up with his mouth on her...

'You'll see here, Miss Winters, that your wardrobe is fully stocked with clothes from our finest designers.'

Kat's cheeks burned as she diverted her mind away from X-rated memories, and her mouth fell open as she took in the acres of sumptuous fabrics hanging in the massive wardrobe. She put out a hand, touching an emerald-green gown reverently, and breathed, 'This is too much.'

But Jasmine was already opening drawers nearby, showing her a vast collection of brand-new lingerie and more casual wear. Everything and anything Kat could possibly need.

Except Zafir's trust and love.

She cursed herself for even thinking it. She might have had his trust, before she'd broken it, but she'd never had his love.

She thought of what he'd said before they'd left Paris, and wondered with a pang if any woman would be able to entice him out from behind the rigid wall he maintained around his heart.

Jasmine left Kat alone after she'd given her an exhaustive tour of the vast suite and shown her where a tray had been laid out with mouth-watering refreshments and a jug of iced water infused with lemons and limes.

After eating a little, Kat explored the bathroom, and was alternately shocked and moved to find that someone—*Zafir*—had obviously given instructions to have the shower made more accessible for her, with a chair and rails.

After a refreshing shower, she put her prosthesis back

on and slipped into a long kaftan she'd found among the clothes hanging in the wardrobe. It was dark gold, and it glided over her body like a cool breeze. She lifted her hair up and off her neck, twisting it into a knot on her head, and went outside the French doors to explore the grounds.

The sun was setting in a blazing ball of orange on the horizon and Kat watched it for a long moment, a sense of peace she hadn't experienced in a long time stealing over her. She took a deep breath, revelling in the heat and the rich, exotic scents around her.

This place resonated deep within her in a way that she couldn't explain. A familiar refrain popped into her head: she came from a trailer park in one of the poorest parts of Midwest America and she hadn't even completed her high school education. She had no right to feel an affinity with this place.

Kat pushed the assertion down. She could recognise how intimidated she'd been before, but of course she had a right to be here—no matter what her background was. If anything, the last eighteen months had shown her where her true strengths lay, and she wasn't as wide-eyed and naive as she'd once been.

She walked along a path shaded by the overhanging branches of a tree that bore small black fruits like berries. It truly was paradise. She spotted a walled garden ahead, but came to a stop at the entrance when she saw that it was untended and overgrown—in stark contrast to the lush perfection surrounding it.

Something about it called to her, and she stepped inside. She could just make out an empty dry fountain, and beautiful mosaics that were cracked and broken.

She felt as if she was intruding on a private space, and was just turning to go when she heard a noise. She whirled around to see Zafir standing in the entrance to the garden, breathtaking in traditional flowing cream robes.

As soon as she saw the look on his face something clicked in her mind, and she said slowly, 'This is where she died, isn't it? Sara…?'

He nodded once, curtly, and stepped inside the garden.

Kat said, 'I didn't mean to intrude. I was just passing…'

Zafir came and stood near the overgrown fountain. 'It's fine. How were you to know?'

He didn't look at Kat, and impetuously she asked, 'Tell me about Sara. What was she like?'

She held her breath for a moment, not sure if Zafir would indulge her, but then she saw the corner of his mouth twitch.

'She was beautiful and stubborn and mischievous.'

'Did she have your eyes?'

Zafir shook his head. 'No, she had blue eyes—like Salim. Long dark hair. They were inseparable like I told you, from the moment they were born. Like a little unit.'

'What about you?'

Zafir shrugged minutely. 'They didn't need me. They had each other.'

Kat didn't know what to say to that. She was blindsided by an image of a young Zafir, always on the outside of his siblings' intense bond, and how lonely that must have been.

'I can't believe your parents weren't affected when Sara died. They couldn't have been so cruel.'

Zafir turned around then, and the cold look on his face made Kat suck in a breath.

'Yes, they could and they were. Don't you remember meeting them?'

Of course she did. She'd met them on her first visit and endured an excruciating lunch during which they'd spoken their own language and made no attempt to speak with her, directing all their conversation to Zafir. They'd clearly deemed the prospect of her becoming a daughter-in-law a total travesty.

Zafir shook his head. 'I can't believe you still retain such optimism about people when your own mother exploited you so shamelessly.'

Kat's face grew hot. She felt like that naive virgin all over again. Mocked by Zafir's deep well of cynicism.

She lifted up her chin. 'I'd prefer to be optimistic about people rather than believe there's no hope for love or redemption. You're not your brother, Zafir. Or your parents.'

Suddenly acutely aware of the small space, and its air of general decay, Kat felt claustrophobic.

She started to walk out, but Zafir caught her by the arm. 'Where are you going?'

She looked at him, and hated the ease with which he could strike at her very heart. 'Back to my room.'

'I've arranged dinner for us in my private suite.'

Zafir's hand was warm on her arm, and it made her think of how it would feel on other parts of her body. It would be so easy just to say *yes*—to go with Zafir to his suite and let the inevitable happen. Her blood grew hot just from thinking about it. But she couldn't. Not if she wanted to walk away relatively intact when all this was over.

She pulled her arm free. 'No, Zafir. I'm tired and I'd like to go to bed—*alone*. I'm here to complete the job of promoting the diamond and Jandor and that's all I'm interested in.'

Zafir's eyes took on a gleam she didn't want to interpret. But he just said, 'Very well, Kat. I'll see you after lunch tomorrow, then.'

She had turned to walk away again before she stopped and asked suspiciously, 'The function is in two days. What's happening tomorrow?'

Zafir folded his arms and looked powerful and dangerous. 'A little sightseeing tour of my country. I'm making up for the fact that you saw very little of Jandor last time.'

Panic skittered along Kat's skin. 'You really don't have to do that. You're busy. I can sightsee on my own.'

He walked forward and caught her arm again, escorting her out of the garden in a smooth motion. 'Your concern for my schedule is commendable—but, yes, Kat, I am doing this. Jasmine will help you pack for the trip.'

Kat pulled herself free. *'Pack?'*

'I'm taking you into the desert for the night—a unique experience, and one I'd hate for you to miss out on before you leave.'

Before you leave.

Kat stifled the dart of pain. She recognised his look of steely determination. 'Fine, Zafir,' she bit out eventually. 'But don't think that this changes anything—all you'll be doing is wasting your own precious time.'

Zafir watched Kat walk back to her suite of rooms, her slight limp the only hint that there was anything different about her.

When he'd seen her standing in Sara's garden—as he called it—he'd expected to feel a sense of intrusion. But he'd felt the opposite. He'd felt as if a weight was being lifted off his shoulders. He'd found himself avoiding her eye, embarrassingly afraid of the compassion he suspected he'd see in those amber depths and what it might unleash inside him.

And then, when he'd told her about Salim and Sara and their bond, she'd asked, 'What about you?'

Her innocent question had impacted on him like a blow to the gut. No one had ever said that to him before—*What about you?*—because no one had ever really cared.

Zafir's hands curled into fists now, as if that could

halt the rise of something dark and tangled that he didn't want to decipher.

He turned around and strode back to his rooms, irritation and sexual frustration making his movements jerky. Damn her for throwing up more questions than answers. Damn her for not making this as easy as he'd expected it to be. And damn her for looking so right here...as if she belonged.

She couldn't belong here. Zafir had closed the door on that possibility comprehensively and for ever. He had a future to build, and Kat was not a part of that future. Very soon she would be in his past and Zafir would have no regrets.

But in the meantime he would use every skill he possessed to make her acquiesce one last time, and then—*then*—he would be able to let her go, and when he moved on and chose his Queen it would be someone who didn't look at him and make him feel as though she could see all the way to the depths of his soul...

Late the following afternoon Kat was in a helicopter, looking down in awe as they flew over the vast Jandor desert. The spiderlike shape of the helicopter's shadow undulated over high sand dunes as the sun set in the distance. It was magical.

Much as she had intended blocking out Zafir's far too magnetic presence, it was almost impossible. The space in the back of the helicopter was small, and his thigh was pressed firmly along hers. And she didn't like the look in his eye—far too intense and determined. As if he knew something she didn't.

She hated that he'd checked if she'd be okay in the confined space before they'd left, mindful of her claustrophobia. At every point where she was doing her best to rebuild her walls of self-defence, he was just kicking them down again.

After about thirty minutes they landed in a small air-field and Kat saw a fleet of four-by-fours waiting. One for them, and the rest for the security team and entou-rage. Zafir led Kat to the first four-by-four, and when she was in he got into the driver's seat. They drove out of the airfield and into the desert, surrounded on all sides by nothing but sand and massive dunes.

Kat was surprised to feel a sense of liberation—as if there was nothing but this in the world. She looked at Zafir's proud profile and the inevitable stubble shadow-ing his jaw. She wanted to reach out and touch it but she kept her hands to herself.

'How do you know where to go?'

Zafir looked up to where the sun was lowering in the sky. 'The position of the sun tells me where to go…and this…' He tapped at a navigation dial on the dashboard. He glanced at her. 'I know this place like the back of my hand. I used to come here a lot as a teenager.'

Kat turned to face him more, curious. 'What did you do out here?'

Zafir looked away and shrugged. 'Dune racing with my bodyguards. Meeting the nomads and hearing their stories. Learning how to fight and shoot. Training my peregrine falcon.'

Kat didn't say it, but she thought it: he'd obviously done all that alone. Her heart ached in spite of her best efforts.

Gradually she could make out a shape in the distance. She squinted, wondering if she was hallucinating, but it got bigger and bigger until she could see that it was green and lush. Trees… A circle of tall palm trees… An oasis!

She'd been to oases before, for fashion shoots, but they had invariably been close to cities. Not like this, in the middle of an ocean of sand, with nothing as far as the eye could see except sky.

When they stopped she got out of the four-by-four, shading her eyes against the setting sun that was burnishing everything red and gold. She stepped forward to join Zafir, who was rounding the bonnet, and stumbled in the sand, her leg momentarily stuck in the soft surface. Before she could take another step Zafir had caught her and swung her up into his arms.

Kat hated how breathless it made her when Zafir lifted her into his arms, and she huffed against his shoulder. 'I hate this aspect of my disability—that I can't just walk where I used to and that I'm so portable.'

Zafir snorted inelegantly. *'Disability?* I've never met anyone more able in my life!'

Kat's chest swelled, and she hated him at that moment for making it so hard to resist him or to stay cool towards him. She felt hot all over now, and it had nothing to do with the temperature of the desert and everything to do with that inner fire Zafir stoked so effortlessly.

The oasis was indeed ringed with palm trees, and when they stepped through the perimeter Kat gasped. Zafir let her stand, as the terrain here was more solid, and she looked around, drinking in the sight of the lush green idyll.

The oasis was carved out of a natural gorge that held a pool of crystal-clear water. There was a small waterfall down at the one end, sending up a spray of white foam. It was breathtaking.

There was one tent set apart from all the others, with a tented domed roof and lanterns outside, already lit. Zafir led her to this tent, and Kat's heart was thumping unevenly.

He had brought her here to seduce her.

How could she resist him in this place of pure fantasy?

Maybe you don't have to, whispered a wicked voice that she tried to quash.

When they got inside the tent a few more of Kat's defences crumbled. The interior was lit only by candles, and it was a sumptuous decadent fantasy, straight out of an Arabian fairy tale. An X-rated fairy tale. Because what dominated the lush scene was an enormous bed, on top of which lay jewel-coloured cushions and satin bedding. Or maybe the bed was all she saw because she couldn't stop thinking about sex with Zafir again.

One last time.

She somehow managed to tear her gaze from the bed and looked at Zafir. He stood near the entrance, watching her with that intent gaze.

Even though she suspected she already knew the answer she asked, 'Where are you sleeping?'

Zafir even allowed his mouth to tip up minutely, as if she merely amused him. 'In here—with you.'

He moved into the tent. Kat panicked even as her insides quivered with anticipation. If he touched her—which she yearned for as much as she feared—he'd surely guess how far she'd fallen for him all over again.

She put up a hand, seizing on *anything* to try and remind Zafir that she wasn't worth pursuing. She blurted out the first thing she could think of. 'You've accused me of having no ability to manage money and you're right!'

Zafir shook his head. 'Kat, we're not here to discuss your credit rating.'

She ploughed on, determined to try and make him turn away in disgust. 'The money you've given me upfront for this job? It's gone. Already.'

She waited with bated breath, but Zafir just kept coming closer and said easily, 'It's none of my business what you do with your money, Kat. But as a matter of interest what did you spend it on?'

Kat was deflated. She wished she could brandish some gaudy bauble under Zafir's nose, but of course she couldn't—and she also couldn't lie.

She avoided his eye. 'I gave it to the rehabilitation centre where I went after my accident because they're in trouble. And some to Julie, because she supported me.'

Zafir's feet came into her line of vision. He put a finger under her chin, tipping her face up. There was an enigmatic look on his face.

'I know, Kat.'

Her eyes widened with shock. 'How did you know?'

'Because whenever such a large sum of money is wired to another account the bank checks to make sure it's a genuine transaction. My accountants had to verify it. If you'd told me your intentions I could have given it directly to them...'

Kat couldn't escape his gaze and she shifted uncomfortably. 'I hadn't told you yet...about my leg.'

She pulled her chin free and stepped back a few paces, sensing the walls of the tent closing in around her—but not in a scary way. It was in a way that made her blood leap with illicit excitement. Still she resisted, though.

She wrapped her arms around herself. 'That's why I agreed to the job, Zafir, because I realised I could use the money for good. I wasn't looking for an affair—or an easy payday.'

His mouth tipped up wryly. 'I think you've made that clear.'

He came towards her again, as if determined not to give her any space, and for a moment Kat might have believed that they'd slipped through time to another age, where he was a medieval warrior king and there was nothing beyond this place but untamed lands and fierce desires.

He put his hands on her arms.

Far too weakly, Kat said, 'Zafir, *no.*'

His eyes were silver in the flickering candlelight. 'Kat, *yes*. All that matters is this moment. Here and now.'

His words impacted on her like little bombs, blasting the last of her shaky defences.

He pulled her so close that she could feel his chest moving against hers, and the blunt thrust of his burgeoning arousal. Then he cupped her face with his hands, tipping it up to his, and as his mouth covered hers Kat stayed tense, even though she knew it was futile. She wanted this as much as he did.

She was fooling herself if she thought that denying herself this would make things easier in the end... Or at least that's how she justified it to herself as she found herself softening, tipping over the edge of resistance, responding to Zafir's expert touch and kisses, letting his strength hold her up because hers was gone...

CHAPTER NINE

HOURS LATER, WHEN the oasis was bathed in silvery moonlight, and after they had gorged themselves on a succulent feast and then made love again, Kat was curled into Zafir's side, one arm across his chest, her hand idly tracing patterns on his skin. He felt sated, languid, and at peace.

Peace?

When that registered, a prickle of panic skated over his skin. He wasn't looking for peace. He had peace—*didn't he?* He was just looking for an end to this insatiable hunger he felt.

So why did you bring her here to this place? asked a snide voice.

To seduce her ruthlessly and get her to admit she still wanted him. That was why. And Zafir had felt ruthless as he'd noted Kat's attempts to ward him off. The fact that she'd done it by trying to remind him of the accusations he'd thrown at her before had impacted on him in a place he didn't like to acknowledge.

He'd wanted to stop her saying those things, stop reminding him of how wrong he'd been about her…

Kat moved beside him then, coming up on one elbow. He looked at her and his chest tightened. She was sexily dishevelled and still flushed. His hunger was like a sharp spike, clawing at his insides all over again.

She looked at him, and he saw how her eyes had turned more green than amber and she seemed concerned. A sense of desperation joined his panic. Everything in him resisted letting her see the pit of emotions he couldn't analyse in his gut. And so, in a crude reflex to avoid hearing what she was thinking, he moved, gently disentangling himself from her to sit up and reach for a robe.

'Where are you going?'

Her voice was husky, and even that had an effect on him. Zafir gritted his jaw.

He handed her another, smaller robe and watched as she sat up and pulled it on. 'I want to show you something.'

She came to the edge of the bed and started to reach for her prosthesis, but Zafir lifted her into his arms, saying gruffly, 'You don't need it.'

'Zafir, I *do* need it,' she said, her breath warming his neck. 'I don't want to get too used to this—it'll make me lazy.'

There was something in her voice—an edge that made Zafir's jaw clench even tighter. Especially when he thought of any other faceless man lifting her into his arms. But he was already walking out through the tent opening and across the oasis.

Kat curled into him and hissed, 'Someone will see us.'

'No, they won't. We're totally private.'

He walked until they reached the edge of the large pool, its surface rippling and glistening under the moonlight. The waterfall fell nearby—a muted roar. Zafir put Kat down on her good leg and held her steady as he let his robe drop. Then he pulled hers off so they were both naked.

He lifted her again, and stepped into the pool. Kat clung on and squeaked as Zafir lowered them both into warm, silky water. He held her until they were deep enough to float, feeling her nipples pebble into hard points against his chest, which almost undid him.

And then he asked, 'Okay?'

She nodded.

Zafir let her go and Kat swam a couple of metres

through the satin water before flipping onto her back, her wet breasts gleaming enticingly above the waterline in the silver light.

Zafir's body was so hard it ached, and he swam towards her like a magnet drawn to true north. He couldn't help smiling when he saw the grin on her face, and the way her hair was spread out around her like skeins of silk.

'You like this?'

She flipped over again, treading water. 'Swimming was my favourite part of rehab... For a moment I could almost forget what had happened, pretend I was whole again...'

Moved by something that scared him with its intensity, Zafir caught her under the arms and pulled her into him, so their bodies were touching. 'You *are* whole, Kat.'

Her eyes were huge and unreadable in the darkness, but even though Zafir couldn't analyse what was in their depths it didn't make him feel any less exposed. He knew now that he'd crossed an emotional line that he'd never wanted to cross with anyone, and he was afraid there was no way back.

'I feel whole when I'm with you.'

Kat immediately bit her lip, as if regretting what she'd just said.

The water lapped around them and Zafir gave in to the carnal dictates of his body with an eagerness that spoke of his desire not to think about emotions. He pulled her close, catching her thighs and wrapping them around his hips.

She reached down a hand and curled it around his erection, making him suck in a breath and see stars. *Witch.*

'Make love to me, Zafir...' she breathed.

He needed no further urging. He walked in the water until Kat could rest her back against the soft grassy bank. She arched towards him, offering herself. It was all Zafir

could do not to tremble in the face of such sheer feminine power as he smoothed a hand down over her breasts
and belly.

Catching her around her waist, he drew her closer so
that his erection nudged against where she was slick and
hot. He stroked himself against her body, teasing them
both unmercifully until she was begging… Only then did
he plant his legs wide and hold her steady as he thrust up
into her body, making everything explode around them
and finally, mercifully, dulling the tangled voices in his
head and soothing the ache in his chest.

At least for now.

Early the following morning Kat tried not to be so aware
of Zafir watching her from a slight distance as one of the
senior nomads instructed her patiently on how to let the
peregrine falcon fly from where it was perched on her
arm, protected by a heavy glove.

Her eyes were as wide as saucers as she listened, and
she tentatively stroked the belly of the majestic bird. She
was terrified of this beautiful creature, with its huge tal-
ons, sharp beak and beady eyes, but trying not to show it.

She lifted her arm to let the bird go free, as she'd
been instructed, and it flew up into the air before landing on a nearby stand. The old man with the turban on
his head, the wrinkled face and kind eyes, put some food
on Kat's glove and the bird swooped back to land on her
hand again.

She felt a ridiculous sense of triumph, even though
she knew the bird had been trained for years to do exactly this. She couldn't stop smiling, and looked at Zafir.

The smile slid from her face when she saw his expression. He looked as if someone had punched him in the
gut. He was pale, and staring at her so intently that she

instinctively moved towards him, forgetting about the bird until it moved.

She stopped. The nomad took the bird off her glove then, enticing it to hop back onto his own arm, and when Kat looked at Zafir again it was as if she'd imagined it—now he looked completely fine... Well, except for the intense way he was looking at her.

Memories of their X-rated swim in the pool rushed back, and she was glad of the long traditional kaftan she wore that would hopefully hide the effect Zafir had on her body from these strangers who had appeared to pay homage to their King.

He came towards her, his expression inscrutable. 'It's time to leave. We have a busy day ahead of the function this evening.'

Kat forgot about his enigmatic look as she realised that this was the last function and then she'd be free to go. She nodded quickly and avoided Zafir's eye as took off the glove, handing it back to the nomad with a smile that disguised her sorrow that she'd never see this place again.

Sitting in the back of Zafir's car on their way to the palace, an hour later, Kat was trying not to feel needy. She had to keep reminding herself that their night at the oasis hadn't really meant anything other than a lavish attempt on Zafir's part to prove that he could still seduce her.

And he had.

It was all a game to him. A battle of wills. She had told him she wouldn't sleep with him again, and naturally he had done his utmost to prove her wrong.

Self-disgust curled through her that she'd been so easy. And yet could she regret the intensity of their lovemaking in that idyllic fantastical place, where it had felt as if they were the only two people on the planet? Or the magic of that pool at midnight?

No. Already she wanted to hug those memories to her, like a miser protecting her gold. And Zafir hadn't made any great attempt to engage her in conversation since they'd left, so it couldn't be any clearer really...

She was so distracted with her thoughts that it took a second before she heard Zafir calling her name. She turned her head and looked at him, steeling herself. He was holding out his palm tablet and he looked grim.

'There's something you should see.'

It took her a second to absorb the headline.

The Real Reason Kat Winters Disappeared!

She scanned the piece with a growing sense of panic mixed with terror. Apparently 'a source' close to Kat had told the papers all about her accident, and the subsequent amputation and rehabilitation, with some added salacious details about how she'd wanted to hide away from the world because she was so ashamed of what had happened to her.

Anger flooded her veins...

She looked at Zafir, handing back the tablet as if it was poison. 'I was never ashamed—why would someone say that? I was hurt and in pain, struggling to come to terms with a new reality—'

Kat stopped abruptly, realising how close to full-on panic she was. She'd always dreaded this scenario—the story being leaked—and she realised now that she'd always hoped—naively, obviously—that she would be able to control the story before it came out.

The last thing she had ever wanted was for other people who were in a similar situation to feel she was ashamed to be one of them. She *was* one of them. They had helped her to get through it.

Zafir looked angry. 'Do you know who might have leaked it? Your agent?'

Kat drew back. 'No, Julie is my best friend—she wouldn't do something like this.'

Zafir made some remark under his breath about people and money, and Kat said, 'Give me your phone and I'll call her now.'

He handed over his phone and she made the call. Relief flooded her when Julie sounded as upset as she was, and she hated Zafir for infecting her with his cynicism for a moment, making her doubt her friend's loyalty.

When she'd handed back the phone she said, 'Julie thinks it was someone at the hospital I was taken to directly after the accident. That they saw the new pictures of me and put two and two together.' She grimaced. 'When you lose a leg you tend to be a memorable patient—even if I was using another name and was hardly recognisable at the time.'

Zafir still looked livid. Immediately she thought of something, and her belly sank. 'I'm sorry.'

He frowned. 'What do you have to be sorry about?'

Kat swallowed. 'No doubt the last thing you want is for this news to come out now—before the final event and the last showing of the diamond. It's bound to draw negative press.'

There was a sharp rap on Zafir's window, but he ignored it. They'd arrived back at the palace.

He turned to face Kat. 'There will be no negativity. The diamond will become even more famous when your story of courage is revealed. But I won't force you to go out there this evening if you feel it's asking too much of you. You're the one who will be put under more scrutiny than ever now.'

Kat felt alternately comforted by Zafir's words and bereft. He sounded as if he didn't care what she did either way.

She shrugged minutely. 'It's not as if I've got anything

more to hide than this. It was going to come out sooner or later. If you're not afraid of it impacting the campaign negatively, then of course I'll go out there this evening.'

Even as she said that though, she felt flutters of trepidation—but she also had to acknowledge a fledgling sense of liberation, as if a weight was being lifted off her shoulders.

Zafir looked at her enigmatically before saying, 'Very well—as you wish.'

As if he'd sent a psychic message to someone, his door was opened by a waiting attendant and he got out. The driver opened her door, and when she emerged into the sunlight Rahul was walking over to her, looking pale.

'Miss Winters, I am so sorry. I had no idea about… If I'd known…'

He looked so miserable in his inarticulacy that Kat touched his arm. 'Rahul, you don't need to apologise. You did nothing wrong. And no one knew.'

Rahul walked back to Zafir, who broke away from his attendants to come over to where she was standing. The expression on his face reminded her of the enigmatic way he'd looked at her in the desert before they'd left. It was profoundly irritating that she couldn't read it.

Zafir gestured with a hand. 'Jasmine is waiting to go through your wardrobe and she'll help you choose an outfit for this evening.'

Kat looked to where he was indicating, to see Jasmine and the golf buggy nearby.

Zafir stepped back. 'I'll come to your rooms for you at six.'

Kat wanted to cling to his robes and demand of him, *Where are we now? What did last night mean?*

She watched him walk away and chastised herself. Last night had just been a last slaking of lust. No doubt now that the end was in sight Zafir was already casting his mind ahead to the future and lining up suitable candidates to be his Queen.

Kat shoved down the rise of a very uncharacteristic bitterness and forced a smile as she greeted a serious-looking Jasmine, who was unusually quiet on their way back to the suite. Kat surmised that the news had obviously spread like wildfire.

When they got to her rooms Jasmine looked at Kat with big eyes and asked hesitantly, 'Is it really true, Miss Winters?'

Kat took a deep breath and nodded. Then she sat down and pulled up her kaftan, showing the young girl her leg.

Jasmine sank down at Kat's feet. When she looked up at Kat her eyes were brimming over with tears, and for the first time since her accident Kat felt a sense of liberation bubble up inside her as she reached out and wiped Jasmine's tears.

'It's not that bad, really,' she said with a wry smile. 'Here, let me show you...'

That evening, Kat paced back and forth unevenly across her suite. In spite of her bravado earlier, her nerves were intensifying with every moment at the thought that when she was presented tonight everyone would *know*.

Jasmine melted away discreetly when Zafir appeared at the entrance to her main reception room. Kat stopped pacing and looked at him, her nerves dissolving for a moment as she took him in, resplendent in cream and gold robes, every inch the powerful and impressive King of his country.

His grey eyes raked her up and down. 'You look beautiful.'

Kat felt ridiculously shy and half shrugged. 'Jasmine liked this dress the best.'

It was a long traditional Jandori kaftan, with decep-

tively simple flowing lines and a V-neck that showed off
the diamond she was already wearing. Noor had deliv-
ered it shortly before. Over the kaftan she wore a long
sleeveless robe inlaid with gold embroidery.

She noticed then that she and Zafir were almost match-
ing, as her kaftan was a similar colour to his. For a second her rogue imagination wondered if this was close to
what the bride of Zafir would wear on her wedding day.

It took her a second to realise that Zafir had spoken
and she hadn't even heard him. Mortified, she said, 'I'm
sorry, what did you say?'

She noticed then that he appeared less than his usual
composed self.

He ran a hand through his hair and looked at her.
'There's something I need to tell you. I was going to
wait until later, but...'

Kat went cold inside. 'What is it?'

He was grim. 'It's something I discovered this afternoon—a couple of things, actually.'

Kat wasn't sure why, but she felt she needed to sit
down on a nearby chair. 'What things?'

Zafir started to pace back and forth, exactly where Kat
had just been. He stopped and said abruptly, 'My father
was the one who leaked those pictures and the story of
your background to the press.'

Kat went very still. Zafir's father's cold features came
back into her mind's eye. She stood up again. 'I know he
didn't approve of me... But how...? Where did he find
the pictures?'

Zafir was pacing again, energy crackling around him
like a forcefield. 'He hired investigators to look into your
past. They found the photographer and paid him a lot of
money to hand over some of the photos.' He stopped again
and looked stricken. 'I'm sorry, Kat. I had no idea... If
I'd known...'

Kat walked blindly over to another chair, and clutched the back of it. Faintly, she said, 'You couldn't have known.'

She looked at Zafir and tried to push down the feeling of betrayal, even though it hadn't had anything to do with him. She'd known his parents hadn't liked her, but to go that far was hurtful in the extreme.

'It's not relevant now, anyway. What's done is done… your father is dead.'

'There's something else too.'

Kat's hand tightened on the chair. She regretted standing up. 'What?'

'I tracked down the photographer—or rather my team did. That's how I found out about my father's involvement.'

He paced again and then stopped. He'd never reminded Kat more of a caged animal than right now.

His face was all stark lines and hard jaw. 'You should have told me everything, Kat. You should have told me that the photographer was blackmailing you.'

She blanched. 'He told you…?'

Zafir nodded. 'I wanted to make sure that he had no more images of you, and I made sure that the ones that did get leaked to the press were destroyed. They'll never surface again. He was still very bitter about having had his payday taken away from him when the pictures were leaked and published. You could have told me, Kat,' Zafir said now, with an almost bewildered tone in his voice. 'Was I such an ogre?'

Her weak heart clenched. 'No, of course not. I didn't tell you because I was ashamed. You weren't an ogre, but you were a Crown Prince, Zafir. You didn't suffer fools lightly. And I felt like a fool for allowing myself to get into that situation. So many times I wanted to tell you what had happened, but at the last second I couldn't... I never wanted you to find out. Not even now.'

Zafir's jaw clenched. 'No, you would have preferred to go into marriage bringing your baggage with you—bleeding us *both* dry.'

Kat's blood drained south. This was proof, if she'd ever needed it, that nothing had changed between them. She was still in disgrace.

Kat lifted her chin and said, as coolly as she could, belying her profound hurt, 'That would never have been my intention, Zafir.'

Zafir cursed and ran a hand through his hair again. 'I'm sorry... You didn't deserve that...'

Kat refused to let his apology impact on her and forced herself to say, 'Even if you'd known the truth it wouldn't have changed anything. I still would have been deemed unsuitable. I broke your trust, Zafir. I know that.'

His mouth tightened into a grim line. The pain cut deeper when he didn't contradict her. As she watched she could see him retreat somewhere, become stiff, expressionless.

'You don't need to go out there this evening if you don't want to, Kat. I know it must terrify you, in spite of what you said earlier. I hired you and put you in front of the world's media again, and it was through your involvement with me that you had to endure your career and reputation being ruined in the first place. It's my fault you're under this renewed scrutiny.'

He sounded like a stranger. A civil stranger. Not the man who had taken her into a magical pool last night and made love to her as if his life depended on it. But then she hardly needed reminding of where this had been headed all along.

Kat stepped out from behind the chair. She said, 'No.

I committed to doing a job and I'm not going to renege on that.'

Just then there was a knock on the door, and Rahul's voice saying, 'Sire, they're ready for you and Miss Winters.'

Zafir looked at Kat. His insides felt as if they were being corroded by acid. He felt tainted by his father's machinations.

He was still reeling from the revelations of the previous few hours, but now he felt something similar to the way he'd felt much earlier that day, when he'd watched Kat with that bird of prey on her arm, clearly scared but determined not to show it. *Proud.* She'd looked regal, and it had impacted on him like a punch to his gut.

She stepped forward now, and she was a vision in gold with the red diamond glowing at her throat.

He said, 'Are you sure, Kat? You really don't have to do it if you don't want to. I've asked enough of you.'

An inner voice mocked him. *You asked for nothing less than her unconditional surrender and you got it.*

'I'm sure.'

And then she walked to the door, straight-backed and proud. Zafir battled an almost feral urge to grab her and shut the door—as if he knew that as soon as she walked through it she would be lost to him in a way he'd never really appreciated before.

But he couldn't stop her.

He followed her out to the corridor, where Noor and Rahul were waiting. Kat was staring straight ahead and he took her arm, leading her towards the ceremonial room. She didn't resist his touch but he could feel her tension.

Just before the doors to the ceremonial room opened Zafir gripped her arm hard and willed her to look at him.

After a few seconds she did—with clear reluctance. He couldn't read anything in those golden eyes. Could see nothing but a distance he'd never seen before.

His bleakness intensified. For the first time in his life he was floundering. The big doors were slowly opening, and with a heavy weight in his chest he said, 'I'm sorry, Kat.'

'I'm sorry, Kat.'

Zafir's words reverberated in Kat's head as she wound her way through the crowd, with Noor hovering protectively at her side. She'd smiled so much she thought she'd never be able to crack a smile again, even while her heart was shattering.

When Zafir had looked at her outside the door and said those words Kat had known then that it was over. It couldn't have been clearer.

Their past had been resurrected in spectacular fashion and now Zafir knew Kat's story—warts and all. Clearly he was taking responsibility for his father's actions and felt guilty, but Kat couldn't let him own all that guilt.

She should have told him everything. She should've have trusted that he wouldn't reject her... And even if he had—well, then she might possibly have saved herself the negative press fallout because he might have pursued the photographer earlier to protect his reputation as much as hers.

But she'd been living in a dream...fantasising that Zafir loved her and that she would make a great Queen... until it had all shattered. The truth was that their bond hadn't been strong enough to hold them together.

Then...or now.

For a moment the crowd seemed to thin around her and she sucked in a breath, relaxing her facial muscles for the first time in hours. Zafir was on the opposite side of the room, and Kat saw that for once there were no body-guards close by. She had the crazy sensation that she wanted to run from the room, taking the diamond with her—as if it was all she had left to bind her to Zafir, and once it was taken off at the end of the evening she'd disappear completely and he wouldn't even notice she'd gone.

Kat looked over to where Zafir was and at that moment, as if feeling the weight of her gaze on him, he turned his head and his gaze zeroed in on her immediately. Not wanting him to read her far too expressive face, Kat turned and took advantage of the lull to escape to a quieter part of the room.

She saw open French doors nearby, and was almost there when she bumped into someone. She started to apologise, but the words died on her tongue as she recognised who it was. Zafir's mother. And suddenly everything she was feeling coalesced into a very familiar sense of inadequacy. The sense of déjà vu was overwhelming.

Zafir's mother was a tall and regal woman, with cold dark eyes and a strong-boned handsome face. Her head was veiled and she wore an elaborate royal blue kaftan. Kat felt ridiculously ill-prepared, and found herself doing what she'd done the first time—bending in an awkward curtsey, with the vague idea that all royalty had to be curtsied to. Not that she'd ever done that to Zafir, of course.

When she stood again the older woman was managing to look down her nose at Kat, even though she was about the same height.

In perfect English she said, 'I hadn't expected to see you here again.'

Kat tried to ignore the dart of hurt at the thought of what this woman's husband, and possibly she too, had done. Kat didn't need to be reminded that she was not of this world and never would be. 'Your son was kind enough to offer me a job opportunity...'

To be in his bed.

Kat didn't say it.

But as if reading her mind, the older woman made a rude sound. 'If you want to call it that.' And then she said, 'Is it true what they're saying? You lost your leg?'

'Yes.' Kat stood tall. 'My left leg—below the knee.'

Someone who looked like a personal maid came forward then, and whispered something in Zafir's mother's ear.

When the maid melted away again she gave Kat a glacial once over and said, 'If you'll excuse me, please?' And then she swept off with a veritable retinue of people in her wake.

Kat was left reeling a little at the woman's ill manners. And then, remembering that she'd wanted to escape Zafir, she quickly walked outside to a blissfully deserted terrace. She went over to the wall overlooking Jahor and sucked in some air. Thousands of lights lit up the city, making it look even more exotic than usual.

For a moment she stood tthere, soaking in the view, because as of tomorrow morning when her flight took off she wouldn't ever see it again.

Her peace was shattered, though, when a group of laughing, chattering people came out to the terrace. Kat tensed and turned around warily, ready to project her model persona again.

When the group of about five men and six women saw who it was they stopped, before smiling and moving forward towards Kat, evidently excited that they had a private audience with her.

Kat smiled, but the wall was at her back and the people were pressing closer. They weren't speaking English and they were all talking at once, crowding around her to see the diamond.

Kat tried to look around them, to see if she could see

Noor or another bodyguard, but there was no sign of anyone from the security team and she cursed herself for fleeing.

Someone reached out to touch the diamond and Kat started to panic, her breath growing choppy. They were closing in on her and she had nowhere to go. She couldn't see past them, and one of the women had very strong perfume, which made it even harder to breathe.

Someone caught at Kat's arm then, in a surprisingly firm grip which only intensified her panic and growing sense of claustrophobia. She pulled her arm free and stepped to the side in a bid to escape—and found she was stepping into nothing as she discovered too late that there must have been a step she hadn't noticed.

She couldn't stop herself falling helplessly, and all she heard at the last minute was a familiar voice saying, *'Kat!'*

She had flashes of being held in Zafir's arms as he strode through the crowd, saying angrily, 'Where the hell were you, Noor? Those people were all over her...'

Kat tried desperately to speak, to say something, but her tongue wouldn't work and then everything faded out.

CHAPTER TEN

A COUPLE OF HOURS later Zafir was still experiencing waves of relief reverberating through his system. Kat had apparently not suffered any major injury apart from a bump to her head when she'd tumbled down those steps that of course she wouldn't have seen with that thick crowd of people pressing around her.

His hands instinctively clenched tighter when he re-called seeing her lying there, so pale and unmoving, the crowd just gaping at her ineffectually.

She'd come round soon after arriving at the hospital, and her first concern had been to tell him that it hadn't been the security team's fault—she'd slipped away from them. Her instinct to protect their incompetence had only increased his ire at them. And made him realise how much he'd underestimated Kat's innate loyalty.

Zafir was standing on the other side of a door with a window in it, looking at Kat, who was sitting on a bed dressed in a hospital gown. She'd had an MRI scan and they were just waiting to hear the results. Even in an un-flattering hospital gown she took his breath away.

She wasn't wearing her prosthesis and there was a wheelchair nearby. But she wasn't alone—there was a little girl sitting beside her aged about nine or ten. The little girl was also a below-the-knee amputee.

He couldn't hear what they were saying, but the little girl was looking at Kat with wide eyes. And then sud-denly a hesitant smile bloomed across her pretty face. She'd had tear-stained cheeks when a doctor had brought her to see Kat a short while before.

The little girl's doctor came alongside Zafir now, and

said in a low, awestruck voice, 'Thank you for agreeing to let Amira visit with Miss Winters.'

Zafir desisted from saying that as soon as he'd told Kat about the young girl she'd insisted on him letting her come to visit.

The doctor continued, 'Amira lost her leg due to meningitis. She hasn't spoken a word in months to anyone—not even her family. But now look at her...' The doctor shook his head. 'Miss Winters is a remarkable woman.'

Zafir curbed his irritation that the doctor felt the need to point out to him what he already knew. He was on edge and unsettled.

The doctor pushed open the door and went in to get Amira. She hopped off the bed and got into her wheelchair and waved goodbye to Kat.

Zafir got down on his haunches as she was being wheeled out of the room and her eyes grew as round as they'd been when she'd seen and recognised him the first time.

He held out his hand and she put her much smaller one into his. Something completely alien inside him shifted and expanded.

'Hello, Amira. I believe you've been a very brave young lady?'

She nodded soberly, her huge brown eyes wide with an awe that Zafir was sure wasn't solely for him. Then she said something to him in their own language with an endearing lisp and that alien sensation inside him expanded even more, stopping his breath for a second.

He had to stand to let the doctor wheel her out, and he heard Kat ask, 'What is it? You look as if you've seen a ghost. What did she say to you?'

He turned to Kat, and for the first time in his life he knew that he was being a coward when he said, 'Nothing important.' He went over to her. 'How are you feeling?'

Kat grimaced and put her hand up to where she'd hit her head. 'I think I'll have a headache for about a week, but other than that I'm fine.' She looked at him. 'I didn't mean to disrupt the evening so dramatically.'

Zafir shook his head, feeling anger rise again. 'Those people were practically pushing you through the wall.'

Kat tried not to let herself read anything into Zafir's concern—the way he'd stayed by her side from the moment he'd brought her to the hospital. She tried again, saying, 'You really don't have to stay...'

He shook his head and folded his arms. 'I'm not moving.'

Just then the kind doctor arrived, smiling. He closed the door behind him and came over, saying, 'Good news—nothing untoward appeared on the scan. I'm afraid you'll just have a nasty bump for a couple of weeks, but it should go down in time.'

Zafir looked at the doctor. 'You're sure she's okay?'

'Yes. I can let her go home as long as someone keeps an eye on her overnight for signs of concussion.'

Zafir said immediately, 'I'll make sure she's watched tonight.'

Jasmine arrived then, with some clothes for Kat, and helped her to put on her prosthetic limb and get dressed once the men had stepped outside.

The diamond had been dispatched shortly after Kat had arrived at the hospital—taken by a very meek-looking security guard.

Kat was wheeled out of the hospital in a wheelchair, as per regulations, but once outside she stood up, unsteady for a moment.

Zafir took her arm, leading her over to where his car was waiting.

When they were moving through the narrow streets

towards the palace Kat said as lightly as she could, 'I should still be able to make my flight tomorrow morning.'

Zafir looked at her, and the expression on his face brooked no argument. 'I've postponed it, Kat. You need a day to recover. At least.'

Kat's heart thumped at the thought of another day and night here, knowing that Zafir was just biding his time till she was gone. 'But I'm fine.'

He shook his head, and something sparked in his eyes. 'Is one more day really too much, Kat? You want to leave that badly?'

She was shocked. 'No… I love it here.'

But I also love you, and one more minute than necessary is torture.

But of course she didn't say that.

She swallowed her emotion and said, 'It's fine. I'll stay.'

She turned her head to look out of the window. After their explosive conversation before the event, and Zafir's 'I'm sorry,' Kat knew there was nothing more for them to say to each other. The past had been laid to rest. Now she would just have to suck up the fact that Zafir was acting out of a sense of responsibility. And possibly still that misplaced guilt. No doubt he wanted her continued presence here as little as she did.

When they arrived back at the palace Jasmine was waiting for them, and also Rahul, both looking worried. Zafir gave instructions to Jasmine in his own language and she whisked Kat back to her suite, shooting her concerned glances.

When Kat had had a bath and was re-emerging from the bathroom, feeling a little more human again without half a ton of make-up on her face, Jasmine was still there and looking determined.

Before Kat could say anything the younger woman

said, 'I'm not leaving. The King has told me someone needs to watch over you tonight in case of concussion.'

Kat knew that arguing would be futile. 'Very well...'

She got into bed as Jasmine curled up on a large love seat nearby, her pretty face illuminated by the screen of her palm tablet. Kat felt a surge of gratitude at the thought of how much the girl had already come to mean to her.

Before she tried to go to sleep she said, 'Thank you, Jasmine.'

The girl looked up and smiled. 'You're welcome, Miss Winters. Now, get some rest.'

Kat thought she'd toss and turn for a while, but she actually slipped into sleep almost immediately.

When she woke some time later the room was in darkness and her throat was dry. She struggled to sit up in the bed, and immediately saw movement in the corner—something big and dark. A scream stuck in Kat's throat for a second, before she realised with a hammering heart that it was Zafir looming over her in the moonlight.

'What is it?' he asked. 'Are you all right? Is your head hurting?'

'No, I'm just thirsty. Where's Jasmine?'

Zafir sat down on the edge of the bed and turned on a low light. Kat saw that stubble darkened his jaw and that his hair was mussed up as if he'd been running a hand through it.

He reached for some water and handed Kat the glass. She took a few gulps, hating how aware she was of Zafir's big body. Was it only a couple of days ago he'd been making love to her with such zealous passion? Now he couldn't be more distant.

He took the glass and put it back. His body was rigid with tension and something inside Kat broke. Clearly he couldn't stand to be near her any more.

She sank back under the covers. 'You don't need to watch me, Zafir. I'm fine.'

He reached over and turned off the light and said, 'I'm not going anywhere, Kat.'

And then he stood up and retreated back into the shadows.

When Kat woke up the next morning Jasmine was the first person she saw, and she wondered for a moment if she'd imagined Zafir being there during the night. She was too scared to ask.

Kat ate breakfast, and then took a shower and dressed. Jasmine helped her to put on her prosthetic leg—the girl was totally unfazed now by the whole thing.

She'd deliberately chosen from her own clothes, knowing that she'd be leaving all the other gorgeous garments behind. They belonged to a Kat who had lived a stolen dream for a short time.

After packing most of her things she looked up flights from Jahor to America, and saw that there was one late that night. On impulse she booked a seat, even though her flight home was meant to have been on Zafir's private plane.

She stood up then, determined to go and find Zafir and tell him she was leaving and not to let him persuade her otherwise.

Kat made her way slowly to where Zafir's office was located, absorbing the understated finery of the palace for the last time—its ancient murals and hidden inner courtyards covered in mosaics, and the peacocks strutting around loose and free, as if they owned the place.

When she got to the office she was surprised not to see Rahul outside, in his usual spot, but his cell phone sat on the table so presumably he wasn't far away. Then

Kat heard raised voices, and one familiar one sent icicles down her spine.

Zafir's mother.

Instinctively Kat wanted to turn away from that strident voice, but something kept her rooted to the spot, near the half-open door to Zafir's office.

'What are you going to do about Salim? Your brother is out of control, and meanwhile the country he is meant to be ruling—*my* homeland—is falling into chaos.'

Kat recognised the tension in Zafir's voice as he replied.

'I am not my brother's keeper, Mother, and maybe you should have thought of this a long time ago, when you proved how little we all really meant to you when Sara died. But if it's any consolation I'm hiring someone who is an expert in diplomatic relations to help oversee Salim's accession to the throne in Tabat.'

His mother sniffed and said ungraciously, 'That's something, at least.'

Kat's heart clenched for Zafir and his siblings, and then his mother changed tack.

'And what is *she* still doing here? Wasn't she meant to be gone this morning?'

Kat's heart stopped.

There seemed to be a year of silence before Zafir said coldly, 'I presume you're referring to Kat Winters?'

His mother made a rude sound. 'If you're thinking of making her your Queen again, then you've learnt nothing about being a King, Zafir. She is the most singularly unsuitable woman to be Queen of this country. There's her scandalous past to think of—not to mention the fact that she made a complete fool of herself last night and ruined the event!'

Kat somehow managed to take in some oxygen at that point. She whirled around and walked away as fast as she could—before she could hear Zafir assure his mother that of course he wouldn't be making Kat his Queen. She tried not to feel hurt at what Zafir's mother had said, but it was hard when it echoed her own deepest insecurities.

She didn't see Rahul until it was too late and they collided. Kat said sorry and kept going, terrified that he'd see how upset she was.

When she got back to her rooms she was glad to find them empty, and was relieved she'd gone ahead and booked that plane ticket. She continued packing, telling herself she'd go to the airport early. She would wait there.

'What are you doing?'

She whirled around at the deep and familiar voice, holding some trousers up to her chest. Zafir was inside her room, the door closed behind him. He was clean-shaven now, making Kat suspect again that she'd dreamt his presence during the night. He was the *King*! And she was now his inconvenient ex-mistress. Of course he hadn't been there.

She turned around again and forced her voice to sound cool. Unconcerned. 'I'm packing. I've booked a commercial flight home tonight, Zafir, there's no need for me to prolong my stay.'

He came over and took her arm, turning her to face him. 'You said you'd stay another day.'

She pulled free and let the trousers fall to the floor, stepping back. 'I'm fine. I don't need to stay—and you have stuff to do.' She cringed inwardly at *stuff*.

'I want to talk to you.'

Something illicit fluttered in Kat's belly. 'What is there to talk about? I think we've said everything that needs to be said.'

'Rahul told me he bumped into you outside my office just now… You obviously came to talk to me. Why did you leave?'

Kat glanced away. 'You were busy.'

'I suspected as much,' he breathed. 'How much did you hear of my conversation with my mother, Kat?'

She looked back at Zafir and pain scored her insides. She backed away further. He was too close. 'I heard enough,' she said painfully. 'I didn't stick around to hear you agree with her assessment that I'm entirely unsuitable.'

A flush stained Zafir's cheeks. 'Dammit, Kat, you are *not* unsuitable.' Then he stopped. 'You didn't hear what I said to her?'

You are not unsuitable.

She cursed her silly heart for leaping at that. Kat wanted to look anywhere but at him, but she couldn't look away. He was like the sun—blinding and devastating.

She lifted her chin. 'No. I told you. I'd heard enough.'

'So you didn't hear me tell her that I've no intention of letting you go anywhere?'

She just looked at Zafir, her brain moving sluggishly. A tangled mass of sensations roiled in her gut, but worst of all was a kernel of something that felt awfully like hope.

Kat refused to give in to it. 'Why would you want to keep me here? Our liaison is over.'

Zafir stepped closer to her, his eyes intense. 'Is it?'

Kat felt flustered. 'Well, of course it is. It was never going to last beyond this job, and you couldn't have made it more clear after our conversation yesterday that whatever was there is gone...' Kat was breathing jaggedly and tried to compose herself.

Zafir grimaced. 'When I found out about my father... Kat, it was a huge shock. It made me realise how badly I'd judged you...how badly I'd disrupted your life. But it hasn't changed how much I want you. Do you know how hard it was for me not to touch you last night?'

His words were like a punch in the gut. She breathed, 'So you *were* there...'

He frowned. 'Of course I was—who else would it have been?'

Kat shook her head and muttered, 'I thought it was a dream.'

She took another step back, putting her arms around herself. 'So...you're saying you still...' She trailed off.

Zafir nodded and his mouth compressed. 'I don't think I'll ever *not* want you, Kat.'

Something painful gripped her insides. 'So what are you suggesting, Zafir? Are you going to lock me in your harem and make a carnal visit when you feel the urge, while you marry your suitable bride and have a legion of heirs?'

'What are you talking about? There's no such thing as a harem here and there hasn't been for years.'

Mortified, because she was giving herself away spectacularly, she looked away, wishing she had something to hold on to. 'Forget it.'

Zafir came close and put a hand to her chin, forcing her to look at him. He had a fierce light in his eye. 'Do you really think that I would want to set you up as my mistress?'

She swallowed. 'I don't know what to think any more.'

Zafir shook his head. 'I don't want a mistress, Kat. I want a wife—a Queen.'

The pain was excruciating. She pulled away from Zafir and somehow managed to say, 'And that's what you deserve. I'm sure you'll choose the perfect Queen.'

Zafir folded his arms. His eyes were like laser beams now. 'I've already chosen her.'

Kat looked at him and felt a surge of jealousy at the thought of this mystery woman. 'Then how can you not let me go? I can't be here now—it's unconscionable.'

Zafir shook his head. 'It's very consciable, actually, because I want you to be my Queen, Kat. And *that's* what I told my mother—before I told her to get out of my sight and that I wanted her gone from Jandor within a week. She's no longer welcome.'

Kat shook her head. Something was happening inside her…something was cracking open… But she couldn't let it. There was too much at stake, too much not yet said. Too much had happened in the past. There had been too much hurt.

'You wanted to make me your Queen before, so what's changed, Zafir? Is it the fact that the truth of my history is a little more palatable? Or is it because you feel guilty that your father interfered? It doesn't change the fact that I did keep things from you. I'm just as guilty for what happened.'

Zafir looked pale now. 'No, it's not because your history is more palatable, or because of the guilt I feel— which I don't think I'll ever *un*feel.' He said heavily, 'The truth is that I didn't fight hard enough for you before.'

'Because you didn't really want to marry me.'

Kat was trying desperately to get Zafir to admit that he didn't really mean what he said. Because if she believed him and he didn't…she'd never recover.

He looked at her for a long time. And even trapped under that intense gaze Kat couldn't help but be acutely aware of his powerfully lean body in dark trousers and a white shirt.

After a long moment he said, 'I can't deny that.'

She sucked in a painful breath. She hadn't actually expected to hear him agree with her, and it should have been a relief but it wasn't.

'But not because of why you're thinking, Kat.'

Kat's circling thoughts came to a halt.

'I was very careful to keep my feelings for you superficial, Kat. I had you on a pedestal as this perfect paragon of beauty and morality—a small-town girl who had worked hard to get where she was. A woman who was unbelievably innocent. I put you in a box and I didn't look any deeper. I know it sounds crazy, and contradictory, but by proposing to you and convincing myself it was for those shallow reasons, I was able to keep you with me while not admitting the depth of my emotions—the real reason I wanted to marry you. Because I loved you. You see, I told myself I'd never allow love to impact my life. I was so sure that I wouldn't ever succumb to such an emotion that I arrogantly denied to myself that I felt anything deeper than liking and respect for you.'

Kat wasn't sure she could speak now, even if she wanted to.

Zafir grimaced. 'When those headlines surfaced and I confronted you... I didn't really give you a chance to explain your side because on some cowardly level it was easier for me to break the engagement and tell you I didn't love you than to admit how I really felt. How could I? When I wouldn't even admit it to myself?'

Zafir stepped closer to Kat.

'I love you, Kat. I know that now, and I always did... I was just too scared to admit it before. Seeing how Salim was so destroyed after Sara's death, feeling that loss myself—it terrified me. I never wanted to love someone so much that it would send my life into a tailspin if something happened to them. And our parents hardly provided us with any kind of healthy example...'

He shook his head, his face paling.

'But when I saw you on the ground last night, lying so still, I realised then that it would be far worse if I'd never told you how I felt than if I'd tried to protect myself from the pain. Even if you don't love me.'

Kat couldn't breathe. She felt as if she was hanging

over a huge abyss by a thread. But as she looked at Zafir, into those slate-grey eyes, the light in them died and he took a step back.

Before she could reach out or say anything he said, 'There's something I've suspected for a while, but I've been too afraid to ask…'

'What?' she managed to croak out.

'The accident…it happened that night, didn't it? The night we fought.'

Kat felt the blood drain from her face, and Zafir's own face paled even more. She'd never seen him look so stricken.

'Kat…what did I do to you?'

He backed away even further, as if he couldn't bear to be near her. Everything in her rebelled at that. He'd told her he loved her. She had to believe. To trust.

She closed the distance between them and took his hands in hers. They felt cold. 'No,' she said, and then more firmly, when she saw his eyes so bleak, '*No*, Zafir. You do not get to do this. What happened that night was no one's fault. It could have just as easily been you. You don't get to take responsibility for an accident.'

She clung onto his hands, willing him to come back to her.

'I was an emotional coward too… As soon as I heard you say you didn't love me I ran—because I wasn't brave enough to fight for myself or for you.'

He shook his head, his face etched with pain. 'I have no right to ask you to stay now. I've brought nothing but destruction into your life.'

He wouldn't look at her, so Kat let one hand go and reached up to touch Zafir's face, smoothing the lines, the tension in his jaw. She turned his face until their eyes met and she said, 'Well, tough, because I'm not going any-where—unless you didn't mean any of what you said?'

Fire flashed in his eyes and Kat breathed a sigh of relief.

'Of course I meant what I said.'

She took a deep breath. 'I love you too, Zafir. What I felt for you before was immature… I couldn't handle it. It was too much. I don't think either of us were ready to deal with the enormity of how we felt. It killed me to think you'd only valued me for my physical attributes. I felt worthless. I felt like no one had ever really loved me for me—not even my mother.'

Zafir reached out and cupped Kat's jaw. His eyes were suspiciously bright.

'I love all of you, Kat—every bit. I love the little girl who was pushed out in front of cameras and lights at far too young an age. I love the young teenager who struggled to protect her mother and who did something radical to keep her mother alive because she had no other choice. I love the young woman who didn't let her experiences make her bitter, but who clung on to something good in spite of being blackmailed by an arch manipulator… And I love the woman who overcame a massive life event to become even stronger and more proud. You have a huge life ahead of you, and you're going to be an inspiration to so many people.'

Zafir got down on one knee in front of Kat and she stopped breathing. He pulled a black box out of his pocket and looked ridiculously nervous. He opened it to reveal a square-shaped Art Deco ring, with a red stone surrounded by white diamonds.

'Is that…?' She couldn't even finish the question.

Zafir nodded, his eyes on her as he took the ring out of the box. 'It's part of the Heart of Jandor red diamond. My great-grandfather had it made for my great-grandmother out of an offcut of the original stone. It wasn't her engagement ring, but she wore it every day. I wanted to give you a different ring, Kat. To symbolise a fresh start... That is...if you'll have me?'

Kat's chest had swelled so much that her eyes stung. She felt as if she might float away, but Zafir was anchoring her to the ground, waiting for her answer.

At the last moment old insecurities surfaced. 'What if your mother is right, Zafir? I'm not cut out to be Queen... I'll let you down...'

Zafir stood up, looking fierce. 'You will make a great Queen, Kat. You're compassionate and passionate. You're intelligent and endlessly kind—and stronger than anyone else I know. Jasmine adores you and Rahul would die for you. When I saw you holding that falcon you humbled me with your innate grace. It was then that I knew I couldn't let you go. And then I found out about my father and I knew I had no right to ask anything more of you. Do you want to know what Amira said to me at the hospital?'

Kat nodded, feeling overwhelmed at everything he was saying, each word soothing the wounds of her soul.

'She said to me, "Your Queen is beautiful," and she was right. You are beautiful—inside and out. My mother was born and bred to be Queen and she spread nothing but pain and misery... You are more of a Queen than she could ever be.'

Kat eventually held out her hand and said in a choked voice, 'Then, yes, I'll be your Queen. I love you, Zafir.'

He grew blurry in her vision as he put the ring on her finger, and then she was being lifted into his arms and taken over to the bed.

He laid her down and said fervently, 'I need you, Kat, so much...'

She put her arms around him and arched into his body. 'I'll never walk away from you again,' she said emotionally. 'You're my King and my home, Zafir.'

Six months later

Kat stood behind the curtain with Amira's hand tightly clasped in hers. They looked at each other and Kat winked. Amira smiled widely. In the last few months the little girl had been transformed into her normal gregarious self again, with a new prosthetic leg.

A woman stepped forward and whispered, 'Your Majesty, whenever you're ready...'

Kat wasn't sure she'd ever get used to being called *Your Majesty*, but slowly, with each day, it was sinking in that she was a Queen.

She looked at Amira to make sure she was ready, and then took a breath, pushing the curtain aside and stepping forward.

Lights illuminated their path down the long catwalk. They were both dressed in the latest designs from Jandor's best designers for Jahor's inaugural fashion week, with all proceeds from the show going to the global amputee fund that Kat and Zafir had set up in recent months. The fund gave money to all aspects of limb loss, including research into prosthetic limbs.

Kat had been persuaded out of retirement by Julie, but was only agreeing to modelling work that didn't conflict with her role as Queen of Jandor, and work that didn't disguise her limb—and, again, all proceeds were going to charity. She was determined to make her face and her body work for the best causes this time, and she'd never felt more fulfilled or happier.

But then, her work wasn't the most important thing in her life. Not by a long shot.

As they reached the end of the catwalk and Amira twirled around just as Kat had instructed her earlier, Kat caught Zafir's eye where he was sitting in the front row. His grey gaze blazed into hers, and then it dropped explicitly to where the swell of her six-months-pregnant belly was visible under the kaftan she wore.

The baby kicked, and Kat couldn't stop a huge grin breaking across her face as her eyes met Zafir's again. And then she turned and walked serenely back down the catwalk with the little girl.

The following morning the headline on the front page of the *Jahor Times* simply said The Look of Love. And below it was a picture of Kat and Zafir gazing at each other, with her hand protectively cradling the swell of her belly.

Zafir threw down the newspaper and turned to face Kat, where she lay in bed. He splayed a big hand possessively over her naked pregnant belly and Kat rolled her eyes when the baby kicked.

She grumbled good-naturedly, 'It's already two against one...'

Zafir pulled Kat close and smoothed his hand down her body until he found her left thigh. He lifted it up so that the centre of his body came into contact with the centre of hers. She gasped when she felt him, hard and ready.

'No, my love...' he said huskily. 'It'll never be two against one. It's going to be three against the world...' He bent his head and kissed her before lifting his mouth for a second to say, 'And then four...' Another kiss. 'And then five...'

Kat huffed out a chuckle that turned into a moan of pleasure as Zafir angled his body against hers in a very intimate way. She gripped his shoulders and bit her lip, and whispered as he filled her with a smooth thrust, 'I love you, Zafir...'

He kissed her again. 'And I love you...for ever.'

* * * * *

DEDICATION

I'd like to dedicate this story and give huge thanks to Peggy Chenoweth, who runs the website AmputeeMommy.com. I thank her for her kind patience and her answers to my questions. Her website and blog are an invaluable resource for anyone seeking information and/or support around being an amputee. Any inaccuracies relating to Kat's limb loss in this story are purely my own.

If you enjoyed
A DIAMOND FOR THE SHEIKH'S MISTRESS
why not explore these other
Abby Green stories?

AN HEIR TO MAKE A MARRIAGE
MARRIED FOR THE TYCOON'S EMPIRE
CLAIMED FOR THE DE CARRILLO TWINS

Available now!

MILLS & BOON®
Hardback – November 2017

ROMANCE

The Italian's Christmas Secret	Sharon Kendrick
A Diamond for the Sheikh's Mistress	Abby Green
The Sultan Demands His Heir	Maya Blake
Claiming His Scandalous Love-Child	Julia James
Valdez's Bartered Bride	Rachael Thomas
The Greek's Forbidden Princess	Annie West
Kidnapped for the Tycoon's Baby	Louise Fuller
A Night, A Consequence, A Vow	Angela Bissell
Christmas with Her Millionaire Boss	Barbara Wallace
Snowbound with an Heiress	Jennifer Faye
Newborn Under the Christmas Tree	Sophie Pembroke
His Mistletoe Proposal	Christy McKellen
The Spanish Duke's Holiday Proposal	Robin Gianna
The Rescue Doc's Christmas Miracle	Amalie Berlin
Christmas with Her Daredevil Doc	Kate Hardy
Their Pregnancy Gift	Kate Hardy
A Family Made at Christmas	Scarlet Wilson
Their Mistletoe Baby	Karin Baine
The Texan Takes a Wife	Charlene Sands
Twins for the Billionaire	Sarah M. Anderson

1017 GEN STD HB

MILLS & BOON®
Large Print – November 2017

ROMANCE

HISTORICAL

MEDICAL

GEN STD LP

MILLS & BOON®
Hardback – December 2017

ROMANCE

His Queen by Desert Decree	Lynne Graham
A Christmas Bride for the King	Abby Green
Captive for the Sheikh's Pleasure	Carol Marinelli
Legacy of His Revenge	Cathy Williams
A Night of Royal Consequences	Susan Stephens
Carrying His Scandalous Heir	Julia James
Christmas at the Tycoon's Command	Jennifer Hayward
Innocent in the Billionaire's Bed	Clare Connelly
Snowed in with the Reluctant Tycoon	Nina Singh
The Magnate's Holiday Proposal	Rebecca Winters
The Billionaire's Christmas Baby	Marion Lennox
Christmas Bride for the Boss	Kate Hardy
Christmas with the Best Man	Susan Carlisle
Navy Doc on Her Christmas List	Amy Ruttan
Christmas Bride for the Sheikh	Carol Marinelli
Her Knight Under the Mistletoe	Annie O'Neil
The Nurse's Special Delivery	Louisa George
Her New Year Baby Surprise	Sue MacKay
His Secret Son	Brenda Jackson
Best Man Under the Mistletoe	Jules Bennett

MILLS & BOON®
Large Print – November 2017

ROMANCE

HISTORICAL

MEDICAL

MILLS & BOON®

Why shop at millsandboon.co.uk?

Each year, thousands of romance readers find their perfect read at millsandboon.co.uk. That's because we're passionate about bringing you the very best romantic fiction. Here are some of the advantages of shopping at www.millsandboon.co.uk:

* **Get new books first**—you'll be able to buy your favourite books one month before they hit the shops

* **Get exclusive discounts**—you'll also be able to buy our specially created monthly collections, with up to 50% off the RRP

* **Find your favourite authors**—latest news, interviews and new releases for all your favourite authors and series on our website, plus ideas for what to try next

* **Join in**—once you've bought your favourite books, don't forget to register with us to rate, review and join in the discussions

Visit **www.millsandboon.co.uk**
for all this and more today!